D0651208

HEAR THE WOLVES

SCHOLASTIC INC.

ISBN 978-1-338-26716-7

12 11 10 9 8 7 6 5 4 3 2   18 19 20 21 22 23

Printed in the U.S.A.   40

Originally published in hardcover by Scholastic Press, April 2017

This edition first printing, September 2018

Book design by Nina Goffi

For RYAN —
i'D BRAVE THE WOODS,
AND THE WOLVES,
FOR YOU.
YOU HAVE MY
HEART.

Not long ago, our forest ranger, Teddy Wade, declared that there were three pups to every one adult wolf bordering our small township of Rusic, Alaska. Nearly twice the pups we see each spring. He said it was the residents' respect for wildlife that led to the wolves' rising population. We should have known then, when that piece of news was shared neighbor-to-neighbor over black coffee and fried eggs, that we weren't long for this frostbitten world.

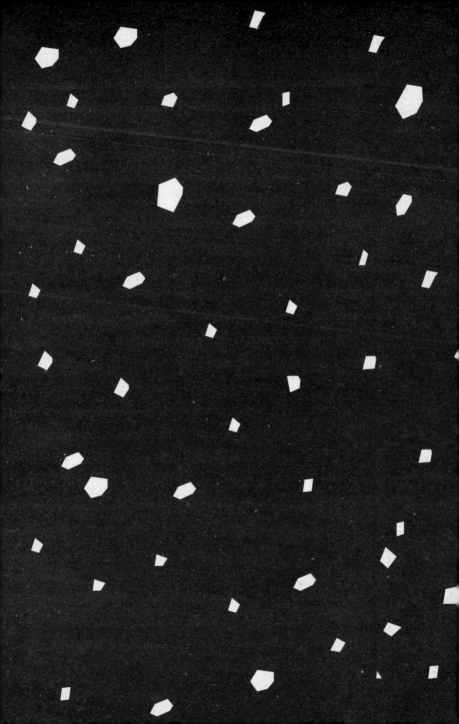

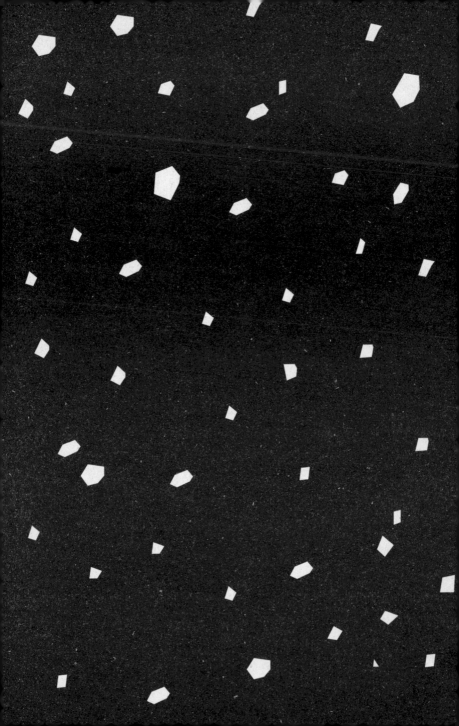

CHAPTER ONE

The circle of life isn't a circle at all. It's a straight line, with hunters on one end, and prey on the other. With my father's rifle in my hands, there's no question where I fall.

I butt the gun against my right shoulder, and squeeze my left eye shut. Snowshoe hares scurry along the newly plowed field, seeking some semblance of the home they lost.

It's the snow. It's unpredictable this time of year. Early October, so our land is merely dotted in white, as if a giant tipped a salt shaker, sprinkled some into the palm of his hand, and tossed it over his shoulder onto Rusic, Alaska, for superstition's sake.

The rabbits are a grayish-brown during the summer months, but turn white during winter. The change camouflages them during a time when predators are ravenous and desperate. When the snow is sparse though, it has the opposite effect. Like chalk strokes on a blackboard, the rabbits can be seen from my bedroom window with ease. And through the scope of this .22 magnum rifle, they're as visible as the sun.

My father looms at the opposite end of the field, and every step he takes causes a flurry of fur in my direction. You can't hunt snowshoes like you can cottontails. They hear you coming, and they flee. If you want a belly full of rabbit stew, you have to sneak up on them, or drive them into the open.

I line up my shot, zero in on a rabbit that's larger than the rest. Take a deep breath and hold it. The blast rings through the dusk. I don't miss the shot. I rarely do. Maybe it's because I'm the daughter of a huntsman and butcher. But I think it's more than that. I can't cook well like my sister, and even Mr. Foster, our sole teacher in Rusic, admits I'm better at killing than I am arithmetic or writing longhand.

It's my father's likeness that steadies my hand while hunting. But it's my mother who reminds me there's an art to everything we do. Whispering in my ear that the rabbit's death gives life. This rabbit means dinner for my family. And his brothers and sisters mean Dad will have something to sell outside our house. He'll string skinned hares and red squirrels and Old World quail from the porch, and the people of Rusic will trade for them. Or, if we're lucky, offer actual cash.

"Sloan, did you hear me?" my father asks.

He sounds as if he's speaking from beneath the river thirty miles east, but when I turn, I find he's a mere step away. I tug on my left ear and stand, take the snowshoe from him. The rabbit's body is warm between my hands, even through insulated gloves. I thread a line through its back leg and add it to the others, avoiding the animal's unseeing gaze.

"I can't imagine we'd need more than this," I say. "It's double what we brought last year."

My father doesn't respond. His brown eyes study the horizon as he scratches at his heavy beard. He shifts his weight, and I notice his opposite hand twitching nervously at his side. But that can't be right. My father wouldn't understand the meaning of the word *nervous* if someone bathed him in honey and dropped him in black-bear territory.

I narrow my eyes and inspect the color that glows from my father's skin. Green. A serious, dark green like pine needles clinging stubbornly to winter branches. His color is a solid, steady shade. Not warm, but reliable. And that's what matters most.

He doesn't really glow. I know that. But assigning people a color helps to sort them. Helps to know what to expect of 'em. It takes me a little figuring to decide what color to give someone, but once it's done, it's done. The colors never change.

"Let's get back to the house," he responds gruffly. "I've got packing left to do."

I should tell him now that I don't want to go to Vernon. I'm not near old enough to vote to keep our townships separate anyway. And last year my sister, Maren, complained the entire time about my clinging to her, and that only reminded me of the year before, when I didn't need to cling to anyone. When I was as free as a sparrow, and as brave as the wind.

Of course if we stuck around, I might run into Pilot. I'd rather remove my own molars than be caught alone with that boy. Pilot turned fourteen this year, and last year his mom started letting him stay behind. I'm surprised she still goes herself, to be honest. Can't believe she'd risk running into that vile ex-husband of hers when he's at his worst.

I stay quiet and follow behind my father, rabbits slung over my shoulder, our boots crunching over patches of snow where the bush once stretched. Now the soil is upended and restless, though it should be used to change by now.

Rusic can be divided into three parts: the woods, the town, and the field. The field is only four winters old, cleared when some people in town decided to try their hand at felling trees for money like the residents of Vernon do. After they downed the trees though, they realized they'd never get them all downriver.

The trees were gone, but the bush remained. Rabbits loved the shrubbery—dense with willow and alder and devil's club—and wolves despised it. And so, in the end, those axmen accomplished two things: They pushed the wolves farther into the woods, away from human eyes; and they created an ideal environment for the hares.

With their new protected burrows, the rabbits began to breed in earnest.

And the wolves grew fat when rabbits ventured outside the bush.

Meanwhile, my sister and I—and everyone else, it seemed—grew more resentful by the day.

The snowshoes destroyed every vegetable garden we had. And they snuck beneath our house and died, creating a stink on the inside. I thought the rabbits had to go. Everyone thought that. There were too many now.

So when Pat Thornton razed the bush to try and grow barley, we celebrated. I watched as he and his men finished the work this past summer, the long Alaskan days making the job a swift one. The bush vanished, the rabbits were uprooted from their burrows, and the wolves feasted until they could hardly hide their swollen bellies behind the trees. And since their shelter was gone, there was more rabbit meat for the taking than we knew what to do with.

If someone wanted rabbit without hunting, they could buy it from my family by knocking on the door. That was how it worked in Rusic—visiting porches, knocking on doors.

That doesn't mean we're a tight-knit community of helping hands.

It doesn't mean that at all.

If it did, it wouldn't have taken my father so long to get me back home, safe, after I ran away. I wouldn't have spent five days alone, in the woods, before being discovered.

The boy who carried me back said he found me unconscious, the left side of my face pressed into the snow. I'm deaf in that ear now, and I'll always hear the world one-sided. My father was furious. First my mother left. And now this.

I don't think he was angry that I lost my hearing.

I think he was upset that it wasn't him who found me first.

Maren is in the kitchen when we arrive, stirring broth over the stove and dropping in hunks of raw biscuit dough. Her blond hair is swept into a bun, bare feet turning blue against the floor.

I drop the rabbits on the table and sit, begin to pull off my boots. "You need to put some socks on," I tell Maren. "You'll lose your toes."

She grimaces, the purple color on her skin dancing. Purple as in unpredictable. Not a bad person, just one you can't quite rely on. A do-it-yourself kind of sister. "What I need is for you to clean those hares."

"There's cleaned meat in the icebox," I mutter. "I have to pack."

Maren frowns at something I said and opens her mouth to respond, but my dad cuts her off with a look. Then his eyes meet mine. "Do as your sister asked."

I sigh, shove my foot back into my boot, and snatch the game. Before opening the door, I glance at my father, hating myself for the silent message I'm sending. His shoulders slump as he rises and moves to stand near the window where I can see him.

"Sloan?" he says before I go outside.

I take in my father's soft eyes and callused hands and the red flannel shirt my sister made him. He looks warm. I want him to ask for a hug. The feeling is so strong, and it comes on quick and out of place.

"You know where we keep the extra ammo?" he asks.

I point to the couch, to the tin lunch box hidden underneath. "Should I pack it?"

He shakes his head. "No. Never mind."

"Dad?"

"The rabbits, Sloan."

I nod, confused by his question, but I've got a job to do that my sister can't help with. She can't stomach cleaning the game, and I don't mind doing it. Someone has to.

As I'm shutting the door, I can hear my sister and father

begin to whisper. I don't want to know what's being said. Not really. People tend to talk behind your back when you've been carried from the woods, covered in blood and clinging to someone you rarely speak to.

As I get started skinning the first rabbit, I peek to ensure my father is near the window, and that my imaginary lasso is secure around his middle. He's there, of course. He knows I can't go anywhere without him or my sister in eyesight. For the last two years, I've refused to be without them. Some people may call that fear. But my mother left me alone in our house. And then my neighbors left me alone in the woods.

So I don't call it fear.

I call it disaster prevention.

As much as I'm dreading it, at least our trip to Vernon ensures I won't be alone for a moment. I'll sip hot cocoa by a fire and stay up way too late eavesdropping on Maren and her friends, and if things go smoothly, we'll return with enough money to get us through the cold season.

I'm working on the third hare when the snow begins falling—gently at first, and then in a rush. As the light seeps away, I check again for my father's green hue. He's still there. I turn back to the hare, glancing at the field where the snow-shoe once lived.

Only this time, when I look, I see something different—

A wolf.

Her gray coat blends beautifully with the soil, though I notice her coloring gently fades as it reaches her stomach. She skips along the ground, chasing a snowshoe as if the two are playing. Between the wolves and my hunting, I wonder how many rabbits will remain come spring. It's not a worry. Squirrel meat can replace rabbit. Or moose venison, occasionally. Or fish, if we travel to the river.

The wolf sees me suddenly, standing in the front porch light's glow. I rise to my feet and watch her watching me. It's a young wolf. Just shy of two years old. There are more pups and young wolves than I can count these days, on the verge of adulthood and growing quickly. They're a product of the field, and the extra food it brought them.

The wolf takes a few quick steps in my direction, and stops. A shiver slides down my spine. Though the wolves have never given us a reason to fear them, I can't shake how this one is staring. Soon, a larger wolf joins the female, and the two race after the rabbit. The younger wolf is clearly the better hunter, though she's smaller.

I watch the hare scurry along the ground, darting side to side in a manic attempt to escape being eaten alive, and I'm not sure why I don't simply turn away as I normally do. There's something about this moment that has me frozen. Maybe it's the fading day. Or that this rabbit doesn't stand a chance without its burrow. Before, the animals were matched in speed and wits. Many times, perhaps most, the rabbits escaped underground.

But this rabbit has no chance.

For a moment, I consider calling out. Saving this rabbit, though I didn't pay the ones on our porch the same favor. But it's too late. The male wolf intersects the rabbit's path, and the female closes her jaws on the hare's neck and shakes her head vigorously.

She shoots one last look in my direction before trotting toward the trees, the prize between her teeth. As the young wolf departs, she travels too close to the male, and he nips her shoulder in warning to give him space. The snow falls over their coats as they make their exit.

Late that night, after I've shaken off the uneasiness from watching the hunt, I drift to sleep beside my sister, listening to the night noises outside our bedroom window quiet beneath snowfall. I hear that same hush when I wake in the night, sweating though it must be fifty degrees indoors, even with the generator running.

I hear that stillness in the morning too, when I realize I'm alone.

When I realize my father and sister, and the rest of the town, have left me behind.

CHAPTER TWO

Fear explodes in my belly as I tear across the cabin floors, checking absurd places for my father and sister. My fingers and toes grow numb, and my breathing comes faster until the walls of our home bow inward. Though my lungs heave in and out, I'm suffocating.

"Dad?" I say, voice wobbly.

Tears sting my eyes as my footsteps grow frantic. "Maren?" I say, as if declaring my sister's name will force her to appear. "Dad!"

When I hear a sound that must be them, I race to the front of the house. The knob is cold in my palm as I throw open the door. Icy air slaps me in the face, reddening my cheeks. My brain buzzes as I search the world outside. I see snow falling, snow whirling, snow covering everything in sight, but I do not see Dad.

I slam the door as a fresh bolt of anxiety shoots through me, my heart pounding against my rib cage. He couldn't have left me behind. Not after my mother took that honor first. After everyone left me for five days to fend for myself.

Sloan, you know where we keep the extra ammo?

I drop my head into my hands and pull in three shaky breaths. My mind replays my sister's frown, my father saying *he* had packing left to do, not *us*.

So he got tired of my neediness, did he? Decided it was time to cast his broken bird from the nest?

I grab our radio and hurl it across the room. It crashes against the wall and clatters to the floor. I open my mouth to scream, but a whimper comes out instead. I hate the both of them. Hate them for leaving me. Hate myself for needing their presence.

It's only after I bend down to grab the radio that I see the note on top of the kitchen table. He must have slipped it underneath the radio so the wind from the door wouldn't take it.

I lift it up and read—

Sloan,

We'll be back tomorrow. I knew you didn't want to go, and thought this could be a good chance for you to remember that you're perfectly capable without your sister or me nearby. This will be good for you. You're braver than you think.

The words are perfectly legible in my dad's handwriting,

but I can scarcely read them for the tears in my eyes. He really did it. He really left me.

I crumple the note and hurl it too, catching sight of a light in the distance when I do. It comes from the chapel's stained glass panels, the ones created by the reverend himself—a holy man with an artist's instincts. It's no wonder that my mother liked the guy.

I can't look away from that light, and the blowing snow. For the first time, I cast my eyes to the ground. A new sort of fear rocks me as I cling to the window frame. Too much snow in too little time. And look at the way it falls. Like it has a score to settle with those stupid enough to stay behind.

I've seen many snowstorms, but a blizzard is something else. The worst one I can remember howled through Rusic the day after my mother abandoned us, washing away her sadness, but not my anger.

My thoughts turn to our generator. Do I have enough fuel if my father and sister can't make it back to Rusic in two days' time with winter reserves? No, probably not.

With a trembling chin, I press my lips into a tight line, determined to fake courage even though there's no one to see. Then I'm pulling on my thermal underwear, long-sleeved fleece, jeans, snow pants, stocking cap, insulated gloves and jacket, and my boots. Already, my heart rate slows. Darkness still dances at the edges of my eyes, but I can focus on this now—simple, physical needs. Feed the generator. Feed my mouth. One foot before the other.

When I stand upright, a softened slip of paper in my jacket pocket shifts. I dig out the Special Invitation and reread the words that invite me—Sloan Reilly—to compete in the Junior Art Competition in Anchorage, and say that my samples were accepted and *most impressive*.

I don't know how they got photos of my projects, but that doesn't stop me from hoping they've seen the flowering clematis vine I manipulated to wrap around the rib cage of a steer skeleton. Or the crushed winter leaves I mixed into my mother's acrylics to paint a spring day, showing half the talent my mom had with a canvas.

I suspect Maren submitted those photos in an effort to pull me from my shell. She can be a jerk, my sister, but deep down, I know she cares. Just not enough to fight my father on leaving me behind.

I'm ready to charge outside, when I catch sight of my father's rifle propped behind the kitchen table.

He left it.

He left it for me to find, just in case.

I turn my back on the relic and brave the storm unarmed.

The freezing temperature slams into me like my family's absence—hard and fast, with just as much consideration.

Tugging my jacket tighter, I power across Rusic. The wind stings my lips and polishes my lashes.

After I enter the chapel, the doors slam closed behind me with an echoing boom.

The quiet rattles me more than the storm did.

CHAPTER THREE

The reverend is nowhere in sight. He's left with the rest of them, but it isn't him I'm looking for anyway. It's the diesel reserves he keeps on hand, and the phone that's in his office. The one my father used to try and find where Mama had run off to. Little good it did him.

"We must be looking for the same thing," a voice says, startling me. I glance up to see my teacher, Mr. Foster, striding down the center aisle between the pews. Almost immediately, I feel the need to stand up straighter. "Did you know meteorologists can track blizzards using satellites and radars? They know where it's going before anyone else. Before that they used hand-drawn charts." When I don't reply, he adds, as if I don't know what he's talking about, "The weather is turning. It may be a blizzard."

Mr. Foster believes I don't have a true thought in my head, and maybe he's right. I can't understand his algebra very well, and I can't analyze poems from the textbooks he brought with him from California, but I could teach him a thing or two about Alaskan blizzards. The man's only been here a year, and he hasn't lived through one yet.

I cast my eyes to the floor, like I can somehow see through to the basement below and the barrels of oil that sleep there.

"I need to haul a barrel of oil to my place," I say hesitantly, my heart slowing now that Mr. Foster is here. He may not be my favorite person in the world, but he glows white. A safe, smart white. A *use your head, not your fists* kind of white. He's stubborn—has one way of looking at people that isn't gonna change—but him being here means I'm not alone.

"Yeah, me too." Mr. Foster slides his hands into pockets of expensive-looking jeans. He's younger than my father, but I still see a touch of gray at his temples. Some of the older girls giggle in his class, and I know my mother would have worn lipstick around him if she were still here.

Mr. Foster gazes over my shoulder. "Where's your dad?"

My cheeks blaze, and Mr. Foster's mouth forms a deep grimace. He's silently judging my father for leaving behind his daughter who everyone knows is a coward.

"I didn't feel like going. He agreed I'm old enough to be on my own for a day or two," I say quickly. "But I'm supposed to call and tell him everything's all right."

Mr. Foster gives his head a small shake like he doesn't believe me. And why would he? My father or sister has had to walk me to school every day this year, and the one before that too. Mr. Foster motions to follow him. "I think there's a phone in the back." Halfway to the reverend's office, he looks at me and says, "I'm not registered to vote, you know. That's why I didn't go to Vernon."

I shrug, because who cares? But I know Mr. Foster *does* care. He's the only man in Rusic who dresses like he's going somewhere fancy, and he must spend a half hour each morning before class getting his wavy black hair just right. I sometimes wonder what that California of his looks like.

When we get to the reverend's office, Mr. Foster places a comforting hand on my shoulder. "Take your time. I've got nowhere to be."

My heart tugs at the show of kindness, even as I remember how inadequate I've felt in his classroom. Even as I hate myself for opening my mouth and asking, "You'll be out there? Because . . . because I'll probably need help hauling that barrel."

Mr. Foster offers a smile. "Right on the other side of this door. Just stick your head out when you're done." I have to look away so he doesn't see the gratitude shining in my eyes.

The door closes behind him, and I grab the phone book wedged between two King Jameses. If I know my father, the first stop he'll make after arriving in Vernon is Hoppy Tobacco. He'll buy a box of cigars he'll save for a special occasion that'll never arrive.

The phone rings in my good ear, my hand shaking as I wait for the store clerk to answer. Above the reverend's office, the snow's weight settles on the roof. How long has it been since I gauged the storm? How long have I been here?

How much snow has fallen since I took shelter in this chapel?

"Yes?" a woman's gravelly voice asks.

No *This is Hoppy Tobacco!* or *Thanks for calling. How may I help you?* The tobacco shop in Vernon is much like the butcher shop we run from our own home. No frills. No small talk. State your business, and be on your way.

"Hi, this is Sloan Reilly. I think my father is coming to your place today? Tall man with a dark beard. He'll be buying a box of cigars. You seen someone like that?"

"Nah, no one's come through yet. I get the evening crowd mostly." The woman pauses. "Do I know you?"

"Please, if that man comes in will you tell him to call his daughter? He'll pay for the line." I *hope* he'll pay for the line. "It's an emergency."

I wait for an answer. When I can't stand her silence any longer, I say again, *"Please."* When she still doesn't reply, uneasiness crawls down my back. "Hello?"

I hear it then.

Static.

"Hello? Hello!" I hang up the phone and pick it up again. Nothing. The line is dead. The room starts to spin once more, so I stare at my boots. Take a deep breath. I'm okay. I'm in the chapel, and Mr. Foster is in the next room.

When I open the door, I find him staring up at a stained glass window, his arms crossed, his head tilted so that he can properly study Samson locked in deadly battle with a lion.

He sees me and straightens. "Did you get him?"

Mr. Foster's eyes widen with such hopefulness that I can't tell him the truth. "Yeah, I told him all was fine." He frowns, unconvinced, so I add, "He's gonna try and get a lift back anyway. He didn't know the weather would get so bad."

The last part, I know, is true.

As if to make up for my father's absence, or maybe because he doesn't know what to say, Mr. Foster points to a chicken near the back of the church, covered in dust, standing proudly next to a vase of silk lilies. "You made that, right? Someone told me all the kids in Sunday school were supposed to dye eggs for the Easter hunt, but instead you gathered all the shells and glued them together to resemble a chicken."

I glance at the chicken and remember the reverend's words to me the day he saw it. *It's the perfect symbol of Jesus's birth and resurrection! Only an artist recognizes art.* He chuckled then. *Look there, now I'm being vain.*

Though his words were kind, he was wrong. I only told my mother what'd inspired that chicken. Said my mind had swirled around our neighbor's hens, around all those eggs, dyed and fried and gobbled up before they ever had a chance to live. I told her those chickens must feel like machines, all their babies lost to people.

My father saw what I'd created at the church, and sighed.

But my mother, oh how my mother swelled with pride.

I always figured I could be an artist like Mama, and one day she noticed me gazing at her painting like maybe if I looked hard enough I could figure out how she made those colors tell a story. She smiled and said, *It only takes two things to be an artist, baby girl.* She ticked off the words on her fingers. *Intuition and vulnerability.*

The next day I asked Daddy what those words meant, because I knew he'd have an explanation that was simple. He looked at me kind of funny, but then he said, *Intuition is a way of being smart. And vulnerable? Well . . . that's like when you're hunting big game, like a mountain lion, and you got to make yourself vulnerable to make the kill. It's kind of like being brave.*

I understood him. In order to be a real artist, I had to be smart and brave. But even the teacher before Mr. Foster never called on me for answers. And Mama took my bravery with her the day she left.

Mr. Foster taps his foot. He's a doer, incapable of sitting still. I can't imagine what being locked inside for days on end will do to him. "Right. So, shall we haul some barrels? I haven't done it before. Do we just carry them over our heads like umbrellas?" He grins to show he's joking.

Despite everything that's happened this morning, I nearly smile, because even though I'm crumbling on the inside, twenty minutes ago I believed I'd float away without my lasso around my father or sister.

Now I eye that same lasso lying lifeless on the ground, and I watch Mr. Foster waving me over with an *it's all going to be okay* nod. Before I can decide whether or not it's possible to secure myself to someone new, I reach with my mind and gather that rope into my palm. I clutch the area between the loop and rope, and swing it gently around and above my head, letting the loop pull away and form a tip. At last, I release, *not throw*, my lasso. I even remember to follow through, just as my sister taught me.

It lands neatly around Mr. Foster's middle, and though I half expect it to slip over his narrow hips and slide down those skinny legs, it fits snug. And Mr. Foster doesn't seem to mind one bit.

I start to breathe a sigh of relief, until the doors to the chapel blow open with a crash, throwing a biting cold into the room. Someone lurches inside as the storm rages over his shoulders, casting snow on his hair, white on black.

The young boy, Elton I think his name is, shrugs off his jacket and leads an older woman into the chapel. It takes me a moment to realize the woman is Ms. Wade.

It takes me a moment longer to realize she's covered in blood.

CHAPTER FOUR

The blizzard wails outside the chapel walls. We've watched the sun set and rise, and the storm only seems to be getting worse. It should have ended by now.

We've left but once, Elton and I, to visit the general store. We grabbed gauze, antiseptic cream, and painkillers for Ms. Wade, and canned food to keep us fed.

Ms. Wade stretches to the side, her face ablaze with pain. She's in more discomfort now than when she arrived, with one hand on the boy, and the other red-stained palm pressed firmly against her middle.

After we'd sat her down, she'd lifted her shirt and I'd nearly gagged at the sight. Four neat puncture holes decorated the place beneath her rib cage, blood gurgling from the top three, and her insides bulging at the mouth of the fourth.

"Basement flooded from the snow again," she'd said between labored breaths. "I was bringing up the tools so they wouldn't rust on me. My first year to stay back on the vote, and this is what happens."

As I watch Ms. Wade now, I imagine her slipping on those stairs, tumbling downward with that pitchfork handle clenched in her hand. How long did she hang on to it? Two stairs? Six?

Either way, it bested her in the end.

Mr. Foster paces the chapel floors, his shiny boots echoing across the wood. He's been like this ever since we discovered how little oil there was in the basement. The reverend must have finally figured out exactly how much he and the rest of the town needed to get through the year. Or maybe he's always short right before the trip to Vernon.

"We won't have heat for much longer," Mr. Foster says, as if it's the first time he's declared this. "The temperature inside will plummet, even if we move to a house and use a fireplace. And we've got to get Norma to a doctor."

Mr. Foster glances at Ms. Wade, and then at Elton. "What about you? Do you have any ideas?" When the boy stays quiet, always quiet, Mr. Foster says, "Christopher, did you hear me?"

The boy flinches, presses his lips together in thought, and finally says so softly I have to bend my good ear toward him, "I asked you not to call me that. My name is Elton Dean Von Anders."

Mr. Foster sighs.

I don't know Elton well, but I used to see him with his older brother near school. In fact, I never saw one boy without the other. That is, until his brother left for college last spring. Now I only ever see Christopher—er, Elton—alone, or with his mother. His mama smiles at anyone who looks her way, and offers a warm, *Praise be to you.* But I've also seen the way she snaps at Elton when she thinks people aren't watching. But I notice a lot of things others don't, I guess. It's part of being a good hunter.

I wonder if Elton feels abandoned by his older brother. Left with a mother who always seemed so proud of her firstborn. I wonder if that abandonment feels anything like my own.

Elton glows yellow like the morning light—a safe color, a cautious color. Though I don't see a color on my own skin, I know my daddy would think I'm yellow like Elton.

I clear my throat and ask, "How you feeling, Ms. Wade?"

"I'm doing okay, hon," she responds. It's a lie, of course. She needs a doctor, but with no running vehicles left in Rusic, there isn't a way to Vernon. Save for one. I turn my attention back to the woods, to the crooked spine that splits it down the middle. There, at the river, Mr. Clive's boat lies in wait. The blizzard may be a bully—burying escape roads, knocking out phone lines, and sending old women tumbling down stairs—but the river is too strong to be bullied.

My heart aches thinking about the last good day I spent with my mother before she left. She'd always had grand ideas, my mom. Some she'd act on, most she wouldn't. But when she announced that she and I should travel to the river and spend the day there, my dad had scoffed. It was too far, he'd said, and we had work to do to prepare for winter.

We did it anyway though. Left before he woke, and set off into the morning stillness. It took us from dawn to dark, but when we woke the next morning and crawled out from our dew-covered tent, the first thing we saw was the river.

Our naked toes swished in the water as we sat on the bank, and Mama admired the ruby ring she'd won by mailing in a magazine giveaway entry card. *Chosen from thousands!* she'd gushed when Mr. Clive delivered the ring to our doorstep. The gold turned her finger green, and the rubies weren't real, but the ring sparkled in the sunlight, and Mama sparkled right along with it. Those rubies were the only connection she had to a world of glamor she'd longed for so hard her heart ached deep.

That day—before Dad lucked upon us and guided us home, angry, and yet looking at my mother as if she were a dream he wanted to capture—she gave me that ring to wear for a little while.

Ms. Wade rises from the lemon-scented pew, making her way to the chapel restroom. She gets halfway before crumpling to her knees. As Mr. Foster rushes to her side, I decide it's time to take action. When the blizzard wanes, we'll still be left with snow too deep to travel through for more than a few miles. No one is returning from Vernon anytime soon, and though it's certainly going to be warmer in here than outdoors, even without the generators, and the store can keep us fed, Ms. Wade is getting weaker, and her wounds need tending.

"I'm going to my place," I announce after we settle Ms. Wade in the reverend's bed. "I need to get a few things."

"I'll go with you," Elton says.

Mr. Foster seems poised to argue, but after casting a second look at Ms. Wade, he says, "You have to be really careful. Being out there even a few minutes could—"

"I know," I reply, pushing down the terror in my stomach as I've done since my father and sister vanished, swallowed by the storm. "We've done it once. We can do it again."

I'll admit, though, that the terror has eased. It lives curled inside my gut, tail wrapped tightly around its body, but I can't focus on it. I have purpose now. Ms. Wade is injured, and I won't leave her unaided. I know what it feels like, after all, to be left to fend for oneself.

"I could come this time . . ." Mr. Foster suggests.

But even though I've never seen anything but confidence on his face at the head of our classroom, I see the uncertainty there now. Elton must see it too, because he throws open the doors to the chapel as a response, and the two of us are pulled into swirling snow. I'm nearly blinded by the wind, but I push onward, Elton's hand gripping my shoulder. My lasso is there beneath his arms, but I have it in place for his sake as much as my own. We lean our heads into the weather and bear down. It isn't until I near my place that I spot the first flash of black against the snow.

There's no mistaking what it is I see.

CHAPTER FIVE

Elton's grip on my shoulder tightens as I catch sight of a second wolf racing across our town. Panic rises in my chest even as I try to stay calm. We may live side by side, but wolves don't hurt our people, and we don't hurt them. Truce.

I know this, but when a snarl rises above the storm, a chill digs into my muscles deeper than the blizzard.

"There!" Elton yells over the wind, and I turn to see four wolves tearing at the deer carcass hanging from Mr. Avery's cottonwood. There's little left to the animal, but still they slide their teeth between the ribs and lick the bones clean.

Elton and I quicken our pace as my pulse pounds along my neck. I focus on my family's cabin, and pretend that if I don't look at the wolves, then they aren't so close after all. Still, when I reach the porch, I can't help glancing back. When I do, I'm frozen in place.

A wolf stands not six feet away.

Sniffing the air.

Watching.

When it takes another cautious step in our direction, and Elton makes a strangled sound, I remember myself and charge toward the door. The two of us rush inside, breathing hard, though I try to keep my composure for Elton's sake.

As soon as the door is bolted shut, Elton gasps. "What are they doing here? Why are they so close?"

I shake my head and watch as the curious wolf rejoins the pack.

"I thought they kept their distance," Elton says, as if I summoned them myself.

"Maybe they just haven't seen us lately." I realize for the first time that I'm cradling my .22 mag. "They'll run off once they realize we're still around."

But the statement rings hollow, even to me. My eyes flick toward the field, and my stomach flips as I wonder how many rabbits have survived the blizzard without their burrows.

Without the rabbits, what will the wolves eat?

I think on the ranching fence my father helped build these past two years, all those rolls of barbed wire forming a half-moon through the woods. It was meant to disrupt large game's migration patterns. Keep them closer to Rusic for better hunting even after the winter ends and they normally return to the mountains. But what about the wolves? Has it kept them from traveling to seek new food?

Through the window, I spot the young gray wolf with the whitish belly; the same one that killed the rabbit only last night. Her teeth sink into the deer's neck; she's playing the part of a hunter though the animal is dead. The young wolf leans into the leader, but is warned away with a swift snap.

There's no question that the gray wolf sits at the bottom of the pack's hierarchy.

"Remember what Teddy said about all those pups being mostly grown by winter?" Elton whispers.

I cock my rifle, and Elton's attention snaps to the gun in my hands. He gives a small smile, heartened by the sight of my weapon. I pack a bag along with the gun, and I'm thankful that Elton is here even though the boy is two years younger than me. I gather clothes, a can opener, matches, a compass, and the ammo from beneath the couch, a jolt of frustration firing through me as I stuff them into the bag.

I tug the strap over my shoulder, and hand Elton my father's jacket. He slides it on as I move to get my mag. When I spot the wolves outside the window though, I stop. My gun is great for hunting small game, but I'll need something with more bite if we encounter an aggressive animal in the woods. Like a moose. Or a bear.

Or a wolf, my mind whispers.

Crossing the cabin, I zero in on my father's gun. He

left it behind so he could be at peace as he snuck away into the night. After all, what could go wrong with a sharpshooter for a daughter, and an heirloom .30-06 rifle for protection?

I hesitate to take it though. My father wanted me capable and strong, for me to simply watch the world for motion and to shoot it, but my mother never wanted me to be just a hunter.

"You view the world with an artist's eye," she said to me one night as Maren snored softly. "I love your daddy something wild, Sloan. But don't let him take that from you."

But Mama deserted us in favor of adventures far away, and this gun is a lot more useful than a paintbrush.

I wrap my hand around the barrel, give her a little toss, and re-grab her firmly around the middle. A shiver races across my skin at holding my daddy's gun. My granddaddy's gun. I always imagined this thing would go in the ground with my father. Never figured I'd become its handler long before then.

"So . . . I can take this other gun?" Elton asks, reaching for my .22 mag.

I grab his wrist before he touches my baby, but in the end, I sigh and point to the switch. "The safety's here. Don't point it at anyone, and don't point it at the ground either. You'll shoot your foot."

Elton puffs out his chest, trying to appear older than the ten-year-old boy he is. "I've held a gun before."

After I double-check that the shells are safe in my pack, and pray I can find more, Elton and I move toward the front of the cabin.

"We need to hit the store," I tell him. "Hold on to me, okay?"

His eyes dart to the wolves, and he nods.

With the weight of Elton's hand on my arm, I throw open the door and we trudge into the storm, the cold stealing my breath. I keep the wolves in my peripheral vision, white-knuckling my father's rifle against my chest.

CHAPTER SIX

We reach the general store, our footfalls hurried by the wolves at our back. Once there, I make my way down the shelves. Shelves that will be full again when the town returns with supplies from Vernon.

"You don't notice how little there is until a blizzard comes out of nowhere," Elton says, toying with a two-way radio.

Though there's more than enough food, my heart drops when I find only dust where the ammunition is sold. How many shells do I have on me? Six? Eight? When I notice the boy chewing his bottom lip, I set aside my own worry and ask, "Why are you here, Elton?"

I heard Ms. Wade and Mr. Foster ask him the same question last night, but he only shrugged then.

The static from the radio fills the silence. Finally, Elton says without meeting my eye, "Told my mom I was riding with Beau. This blizzard can last as long as it wants if it keeps her away."

"Your mom didn't check with Beau's parents before she left?"

"Hmm?"

"Your mom, she didn't make sure you had a ride?"

Elton cocks his head. "What is that sound?"

At first I think Elton is avoiding the question, but then I turn my head, tilt my hearing ear to the ceiling, and pick up what he does. Someone is yelling. Someone is yelling and I know that voice and he is right outside that door.

I rush to the window with Elton on my heels. When I see him out there in the snow, waving his arms, his runt basset hound barking at the wind, I frown. His was the face I woke to after lying in the snow far too long. His were the arms that carried me back to town, to my father.

His name is Pilot.

And I hate him.

"Oh, man, Sloan," Elton points clear away from Pilot, and when I see what he does, my entire body clenches.

A large black wolf trots sideways, back and forth, as Pilot waves it away. Seeing how confident it acts, I imagine it might be the alpha male.

When Pilot's dog ventures too far in an attempt to flee

the predator, the wolf darts in the basset hound's direction. The wolves may not attack us, but they'll claim a dog in a pinch. It's happened before.

Pilot races to his dog's side as the blizzard circles the three players, nudging them closer. The predator lowers its head, and when the dog dashes from between Pilot's legs, the wolf makes a second attempt to claim its meal.

I grab my .22 from Elton, race to the door, and take aim at the sky.

The gun kicks and Pilot startles at the sound. Kissing the rifle to my shoulder, I put those delicate crosshairs between the wolf's eyes and pull in a gentle breath.

Try me, I tell the wolf with my practiced stance.

Not today, he responds, and trots away, vanishing into the whirling snow.

Pilot hustles inside the store with his dog. As soon as we're inside, I close and lock the door.

Then I turn on Pilot. "What were you doing out there?"

"Nice to see you too." He narrows his eyes. "What are *you* doing in my mother's store?"

My face warms, recalling a time when we chased each other around the schoolyard—him a boy who walked to school every winter without a pair of gloves, and me the girl who stuffed a used pair in his cubbyhole. I'm not sure if he knew it was me who left them, but it doesn't matter either way. We grew older, grew apart. Barely spoke until he went and played the hero.

"I'm borrowing supplies," I answer. "I was looking for"—I glance toward the window—"ammunition."

"And you?" Pilot asks Elton.

"I'm with her."

Pilot runs a hand over his blond buzz cut. "There's a lot of 'em out there. I think they're looking for food."

"No kidding," I mumble.

"This little guy isn't exactly a guard dog, huh?" Elton bends to pet the animal. "What's his name?"

"Farts," Pilot answers. Then, with a shrug: "He gets into our cabbage."

I set down my gun and cross my arms. Perhaps I should be relieved Pilot is here. It couldn't hurt, especially with hungry wolves circling. But this boy reminds me of a day I'd rather forget, and if we're going to be trapped together until this blizzard lifts, I'd rather not relive my lowest moment on repeat.

Pilot clears his throat, and when Elton is busy opening a bag of Cheetos and giving one to Farts, Pilot takes a step in my direction and lowers his voice.

"I don't go to the festivals anymore. My dad . . ."

I turn my face away, because I know all about his father. I also know the boy gets in fights. His father gave him that—the quick temper. But his mother taught him about compassion, and gave him a shyness that deceives. Pilot may keep his head down, but try teasing a kid outside Mr. Foster's classroom and see who steps in.

I don't know these things about Pilot because I care. It's a small-town kind of thing.

"You been at your place since the storm hit?" I ask. And what I mean is, *Why are you just now showing your face?* But when Pilot only shrugs, and I recall the wolves, I let it drop. "Ms. Wade fell down her stairs," I say instead. "We need to get her to the doctor."

Pilot scratches his cheek. "No cars left in town."

I bite my lip, and then unload my idea. "I'm thinking we need to travel to the river."

"Mr. Clive's boat?"

I nod, and Pilot glances out the window, no doubt searching for those wolves.

"My dad's got ammunition at his place," he says. "He's got a gun like your old man's. Not the same, exactly, but close enough." Pilot hesitates. "But the weather . . ."

I ensure Elton's not listening before adding, "She's getting worse."

"I can hear you." Elton shakes a length of rope he's knotted for the dog. It's a secure, intricate knot, and I wonder who taught him such a thing. "And, yeah, she is getting worse."

"We'd die from the cold trying to get to that river," Pilot points out.

"Afraid?" I challenge.

"Yeah, and so are you." He sighs, and then scrunches up his face, thinking. "My mom had these shelters built in the woods. She uses them to stock supplies when she makes trips for the store, and in case she encounters bad weather along the way."

I'd almost forgotten that Mr. Clive takes jaunts to Vernon for Pilot's mother. But the man certainly wouldn't help her transport the supplies from the river to the general store. Mr. Clive can't be counted on to do much of anything besides carry the mail and boast that he's the only person east of the Samos Divide with a running boat. At least, that's what Daddy says.

"That's perfect!" I say. "We can stop at those along the way. You know where they're at? These shelters?"

Pilot nods his head. "Yeah. Well, kind of."

"We could leave now," I suggest. "Why wait?"

"If Norma Jean's as bad as you say she is, then she could get worse on the way." He pauses. "She could die out there, Sloan."

"If we stay here, she *will* die."

"I know why you want to help her, Sloan. When your mom—"

"Just shut up." I cut him off, because I can't have this conversation. This conversation only takes place in my head. Everyone knows not to speak to me about this, so why is he bringing her up? The invitation in my pocket grows heavy, nearly brings me to my knees.

"Where is she? Ms. Wade?" Pilot asks. And I see it then—his color. It's a resilient, brave orange. An orange that burns bright, try as others might to douse the flames. I'm envious of that powerful color.

I load more food into my pack and then motion toward the door, indicating I'll show him. Pilot follows me, with Elton and the dog close behind.

We march in silence toward the chapel, our heads snapping back and forth, each of us searching for the wolves.

CHAPTER SEVEN

I'm not sure what's more troubling—the sound of those wolves howling, or the smell of Ms. Wade's wound.

"It's infected," Elton tells her.

"Think I don't know that, child?" she responds.

"We put that cream on it though," I say.

"Didn't do enough." Mr. Foster considers her wrappings in the afternoon light.

"If we had maggots . . ." Elton says softly.

My face scrunches up. "What?"

"Maggots," he repeats. "You can place them in the wound and they eat away the dead tissue. Works pretty well."

I nearly lose my dinner, and Ms. Wade just shakes her head.

"We've got to get you to a doctor," Mr. Foster all but shouts.

"I'm old, not hard of hearing. I've been following the conversation, try as I might to ignore it." Though Ms. Wade attempts to hide it, she can't get through her response without clenching her injured side. When the color returns to her face, she adds, "If you insist on overreacting, then at least let me stay here until you get back."

"That won't work," Mr. Foster clips. "What if we can't return? What if the doctor is tied to other patients in Vernon?"

"Then the kids will stay here, and you and I will go," she says. "No reason for them to come and freeze."

"You'll need someone who can handle a rifle," I say firmly. "Just in case." But it's more than that. My heart flutters thinking about the place where Mama and I camped. I searched the ground a trillion times for that ruby ring that day. But I can't help imagining that this time, I will somehow find it, even beneath all this snow. And when I slip it on my finger, I won't be afraid anymore. Because I'll remember the fearless girl I was the last time I wore it. Before my mother left her husband and two daughters, and took half my hearing, and all my courage, along with her.

"I'm going too," Pilot says. I roll my eyes. Him and that rescue gene of his needed by no one.

"Me too." Elton bites his lip. "I won't get in the way."

The way the kid says it, it's like he's afraid we might string him up to that cottonwood and let the wolves get at him the way they did that deer.

"Yes, we should all go," I say. "Better that way."

"The dog?" Mr. Foster asks.

"He'll come too," Pilot says before glancing at Ms. Wade. "Can you walk okay?"

"Yeah, I can walk," she mutters.

"It'll be slow going out there," he continues. "And we can't underestimate what being out in that cold could do. To all of us."

"I said I could walk." Ms. Wade squares her shoulders, and I see it then—not a fear of dying, but a desire to live. That will be the thing to keep her heart beating, but it's hard to hold on to.

I would know.

Pilot leaves, and returns with armfuls of donated clothing, things the people of Rusic have outgrown or worn thin. They're stored for those enduring trying times.

Well.

"We could go back to our places and get more stuff," Elton suggests, but no one responds.

Pilot loads two packs with what food we found at the store, and offers his basset hound a stick of dried venison. The dog hardly chews before swallowing.

Because the time has come to face cold, hard facts, I take stock of my ammunition. Looks like I've got two rounds in my trusty .22 magnum rifle, and another four in my pocket. Though that gun is my pride and joy, she'll only take down small game: squirrels, raccoons, quail . . . maybe a fox or coyote if luck's on my side. My father's gun, on the other hand, is up for anything. Four 180-grain Noslers whisper of death inside that box, and there's one in the chamber. So a total of five bullets for my father's rifle, and six for my own. If the wolves keep their distance, it should be enough.

After we've dressed in as many layers as we can manage, and Mr. Foster has tended to Ms. Wade's wound, we shuffle toward the door.

"We should stop by my father's place," Pilot says, a tremble in his voice at the mention of his horrid old man. "Get more ammo. In case we need it."

When we file into the blizzard—two days strong and gaining momentum—the wind chuckles.

So you think you can dance with me and survive? it taunts.

It takes ten minutes to reach Pilot's father's trailer, and already I can hear Ms. Wade's breathing growing labored.

The trailer squats in the snow like a rotten molar. The screen door is split down the middle, a blue tarp covers part of the roof, and there's trash littering the area, even with the snow burying much of the yard. A rusted truck is parked next to the home, but one look tells me it doesn't run.

Pilot uses his shoulder to shove open the front door. The first thing that hits me is the smell, and I gag and cover my nose with my jacket. But when I see Pilot's cheeks redden, I drop my hand and breathe through my mouth, mad at myself for overreacting.

Towers of stuff are piled in every corner, and the kitchen is no exception. I can't imagine how Nash clears a place to sleep amid this junk, or how he got his hands on all this stuff when he doesn't have a dime to his name.

"I'll try to find your ammo," Pilot says so quietly I almost miss it.

After he heads to the back, Ms. Wade shakes her head. "Stolen, all of it. And to think that boy lived here for years before his mama found the good sense to leave. He's a monster, that man."

"Norma," Mr. Foster warns, casting his eyes toward Elton and me like we don't know it's the truth.

Ms. Wade opens a cabinet beneath the sink, and bottles clatter to the floor. The old woman frowns and opens her mouth to object, when a crash emanates from the back of the house.

Pilot flies out from behind a curtain that serves as a doorway, and Mr. Foster catches him before he crashes to the floor. I don't understand what's happened until the curtain parts, and a man as thin as a pumpkin seed appears. He's got a hatchet in his right hand, murder smeared across his face, and his eyes set on his only son.

His color is red, red, red.

CHAPTER EIGHT

I've got my daddy's gun pointed at Nash Blake's chest faster than he can blink.

"Put it down," I say, "or I'll put you down." My voice doesn't even shake.

Nash lowers his arm and gives a smile that could skin a cat. "I wasn't gonna do nothing. My boy scared me, that's all."

"Why are you here?" Pilot asks.

"I could ask you all the same question," Nash answers.

The man storms by, swaying as he walks, and I lower my gun. When I turn to follow him, I notice Elton holds my own gun between shaking hands. I reach out, slowly, and lower the barrel. Nod at Elton.

Nash pulls open the blinds covering the kitchen window. "I was supposed to ride to Vernon with Hank. Guess I slept in too late for his taste. Some kinda pal he is."

Ms. Wade snorts because we all know why it was Nash

didn't get out of bed. Hank must have been relieved when Nash didn't show up at his house.

"It's been grisly out there. You guys got something to eat?" When no one responds, Nash raises his voice and throws his arm around his son's neck. "Your daddy's hungry, my boy. What do you have in that pack?"

Pilot looks to Mr. Foster for help, but it's Ms. Wade who responds. "I got something for you, Nash Blake. Why don't you come over here and I'll show you."

Nash booms with laughter. "Woman, you forget Teddy isn't around to back up that mouth of yours anymore."

Ms. Wade's face floods with anger and hurt, but before she can react, Mr. Foster steps in front of her and holds out his own pack. "I've got some dried venison. Help yourself."

After Nash snatches the container and flops down on a chair covered in magazines, I summon the courage to answer him. "We're taking Ms. Wade to Vernon by way of the river, but we need ammo for the trip. You got some thirty-caliber around here?"

Nash talks around his mouthful of jerky, saliva wetting his lips. "Why you gotta go now? Too cold out there to breathe much less travel. In fact, it's getting too cold in here." He waves his hand to indicate his place. "I went to the store for more generator oil, but the witch ran out."

Pilot curls his hands into fists, but keeps his head down.

Nash points at Mr. Foster. "The reverend's got extra oil, yeah? Why don't you and my son go fetch a barrel."

"We'll just be taking the ammunition and going," I say.

Nash's eyes don't move from Mr. Foster. "After I get my oil."

Mr. Foster squirms under Nash's glare, but manages to say, "He doesn't have any reserves." His eyes flick to Ms. Wade. "It's one of the reasons we decided to head out."

Nash laughs and says, "Well, doesn't this just put a spin on things. I guess we're all going to Vernon, huh?"

Pilot's eyes nearly pop out of his skull. "You can't come with us."

"The blizzard will ease soon enough, and the residents will return with supplies," Ms. Wade offers. Her voice has lost its edge. Like she's trying to talk a tornado into changing directions.

"Sounds like you guys don't want me tagging along." Nash raises the hatchet. "If you're traveling to the river, you'll need me for protection. Besides, things are getting pretty dry around here, if you catch my drift."

Pilot eyes the empty bottles on the floor. "You can't come," he repeats. "We didn't pack enough food."

Nash glares at his son and tosses another piece of jerky into his mouth.

"Give that back," Pilot demands, growing bold.

Nash grabs a handful of the dried venison and shoves it into his mouth slowly, a cold challenge in his eyes.

Mr. Foster clears his throat. "Maybe if you went to the store, Nash, and got some stuff for the trip. We could wait here . . ."

The teacher is clearly lying, which pleases me to no end.

A hush falls over us as Nash and Pilot have themselves a stare-off, warming the trailer for the first time since we arrived.

"Don't eat any more of that," Pilot warns. "Not one. More. Piece."

Nash grins. Raises his hand. Tosses jerky into his mouth—
And Pilot charges his father.

CHAPTER NiNE

Pilot throws a closed fist into his old man's stomach, and his dad grunts before grabbing his son's arm and spinning him in a circle. The two slam into the wall before Pilot lands a second hit in his father's side. Lowering his head, Nash tackles his son and takes him to the opposite wall. Mr. Foster tries to break them up, and though I hold my father's gun, I don't dare raise it with the three guys wrestling.

"Stop fighting," I yell instead. "Stop!"

Pilot collides into Ms. Wade and she yelps with pain. That's all it takes to get the boy to cease fighting.

Nash throws his arm around his son's neck, crowing. "You see that?" he hollers at no one in particular. "My son thinks he's become a man." Pilot wriggles beneath his father's hold. But Nash only leans in and kisses his boy on the temple. "You remember when I had to change your sheets every single night?"

Pilot rips away from his father. "Shut up!"

Nash rubs his knuckles into his son's head. "He wet himself until he was eight years old. Can you imagine? Eight years old!" Nash laughs until he can hardly draw a breath. Then he straightens and points at his son, still smiling. "I changed those disgusting sheets. Don't you forget that."

Pilot shakes, and though I know what he wants more than anything is for me *not* to notice, I do. I notice the way his chin trembles as he combats embarrassment and anger. The pulse in my neck flutters as I struggle against the urge to grab Pilot's hand and tell him I don't care. Not about the bed-wetting or his repulsive father or this grimy trailer.

Nash grabs the venison container from the ground, opens the door, and tosses the remaining jerky outside. "There, now no one has to argue over it anymore." Nash throws the empty container and it clatters along the floor. "I'm beat. Let's get some sleep and leave in the morning. We wasted the last of the light."

After he disappears behind the curtained doorway, the rest of us form a plan to the sound of Nash snoring. We can't leave now and risk the man waking up and realizing we're deserting him. So we opt to steal a few hours' rest, and then slip out before the sun rises with Nash's ammunition.

As Mr. Foster and I remove cardboard boxes and a microwave from the couch, I think about the choice we're making. To start our journey in the dark is to risk running into the wolves blind. But to leave in the light of day is to travel alongside something much worse.

I shiver as Ms. Wade takes her place beside me on the couch. Mr. Foster slips into the armchair, careful not to touch the magazines, and Elton scoots close to Pilot.

"You hit your dad," Elton whispers excitedly. "Like, a real punch."

Pilot grinds his teeth, still too upset to respond.

Seeing Elton's face fall, I say, "Someone should sleep with the dog. He looks upset."

"I can watch him." Elton slides toward the basset hound and rubs behind his ears. "Everything's cool now, King Farts."

Elton clings to that dog like he hasn't had a friend to call his own in some time. My heart aches, understanding the feeling. When Elton sees me watching, he offers a cautious smile, and I return it, ashamed at how good it feels to have someone close to my age recognize my existence.

The boy scoots a few inches in my direction. It's barely recognizable, the movement. But I notice it. I do.

The trailer quiets as, one by one, everyone closes their eyes and their breathing deepens. As I look at all these people sleeping around me, people I don't usually talk to, I think about Maren, and how she's always telling me to stop living in a shell. What she can't understand is that I don't *want* a shell. Not anymore. After Mama left, sure. I didn't want to look at anyone, much less talk to them. But as the months passed, I grew lonely, and the kids at school grew nervous. I was the girl who didn't speak. The girl who raced into the woods after her mom left. The girl who spent five days and four nights alone in the snow.

At school, some kids get labeled. Too skinny. Too fat. Too smart. Too dumb. Too loud. *Too quiet.*

It's hard to lose those labels. Maybe impossible. But I'm gonna see if there's another label for me down by the river.

Intuitive and vulnerable.

Smart and brave.

I lay my hand over the pocket holding my invitation. My sister may have sent in my samples, but she won't go with me on the trip. Neither will my dad. He says I'm old enough to fly on my own, especially with one of the contest volunteers. But it's only a test. He thinks I need a good, hard shove to get over my fear of being alone. Maybe he's right, but sometimes I think what I really need is something a bit softer.

Never thought you'd be afraid, Sloan, my father said to me a few weeks after Pilot found me in those woods. *I know her leaving upsets you, but you gotta get over this. You're my Sloan the Brave. Where's that girl of mine now?*

He hugged me then. Only for a moment, but I've held on to the feel of his arms around me for two years. When the invitation arrived, I folded that hug right alongside it and kept both safe in my pocket.

I put away the paper, and even with the sound of Nash snoring close by, I manage to drift to sleep. Much later, when Nash has quieted, and all the world is gravely still, I hear a new sound.

Rustling.

Scratching.

I open my eyes slowly, one at a time, allowing my sight to adjust to the darkness. It isn't until I look up at that blue tarp being yanked aside that I see the wolf—a shadow against the falling snow. The animal stares down from the roof, whining and scratch-scratching at that tarp.

Elton wakes up.

Elton wakes up and screams, and our sleepy trailer erupts into chaos.

CHAPTER TEN

Gripped by fear, Elton does the worst thing he can do in this moment—he flees into the night. With the front door gaping open, and Pilot's basset hound barking, the wolf tears away from the hole and disappears from view.

"What's happening?" Ms. Wade yells.

I'm running for my daddy's gun as I respond. "Wolf on the roof!"

"How'd it get there?" Pilot demands, as if that matters.

"The truck," Mr. Foster reasons. "It's next to the trailer."

I grab my .22 mag and toss it to Pilot. He catches it one-handed and switches off the safety. I race toward the front door as Nash Blake crashes into the room.

"You trying to leave me?" he roars to no one.

When I get outside—snow falling over my shoulders, wind snapping through my hair—I freeze.

Elton stands between two wolves. They wag their tails and lower their heads. Their stance reads as uncertainty.

Elton is scared, which triggers their hunting instincts, but the wolves don't associate him with food. Not yet.

Even from here, I can see how unlike dogs they are. Hungry, wild dogs would be barking mad, working themselves into a frenzy. These wolves are stoic, thoughtful, every move deliberate.

The young gray wolf is steady on one side of the boy, and a large adult female dances on his other side. I'm not sure which is the greater threat.

"Stay there, Elton," Ms. Wade says from the wood deck. "And don't look them in the eyes." Her aloofness regarding the animals has vanished. In its place is a graveness that causes my legs to weaken. "When I say, I want you to take a small step—"

But Elton has lost his mind to the situation.

He runs.

The wolves run.

I brace my rifle against my shoulder, and pull in a breath. The larger wolf lies squarely in my sight, but even as I start to tighten my finger on the trigger, Elton takes a sharp turn and dives into the woods.

As the wolves disappear, I swing the gun under my arm and run. I hear Pilot yelling, and Mr. Foster, he's yelling too. But I don't hear what's being said. I'm racing through the snow. Elton has stopped screaming, but I know he's out here.

My heart jackhammers in my chest and goose bumps crawl along my arms. A shadow flashes behind me and I spin around, terror ripping down my backbone. I don't see anything, but a new noise reaches my ears. It escalates until I'm afraid I may collapse from anxiety.

Ms. Wade is the first one I see.

She holds her side and runs through the blizzard, surprisingly fast despite her age and injury. Mr. Foster is on her heels, carrying a pack and appearing twice as hefty as normal. Pilot races next to him, leading his dog and glancing over his shoulder at his father, who whips past his son with a lit cigarette pinched at the corner of his mouth. Nash Blake jogs with his face turned toward the moon, as if that will somehow make him quicker.

It isn't until I see three wolves running after them that I raise my gun. But there isn't time. The wolves are too swift, and I have no choice but to join the insanity and keep sprinting.

The wolves catch up blindingly fast. But they don't lunge as I feared they might. They simply run alongside us, watching. It's then that I realize they don't want a kill. We're running, and they're chasing because that's what hunters do. But there are five of us within sight, and three of them. They may act aggressively, but they are still cautious animals. And they'll keep their distance if we remind them that we aren't prey.

"We have to stop running!" I yell.

Ms. Wade is the first to obey. Mr. Foster and Pilot are next to follow suit.

Only Nash charges onward.

The wolves close in on him, and now I'm filled with dread that Pilot will watch his father be torn apart. Ms. Wade yells and waves one arm over her head, attempting to scare off the wolves. Pilot and Mr. Foster do the same as the basset hound howls. At last, Nash stops.

The wolves stop too.

And that's when I see Elton.

He stands surrounded by the two wolves that chased him from the trailer. The three additional wolves circle the boy, tempting him to run.

Nash takes off toward us, abandoning Elton.

I raise my father's gun and step forward. One footfall after another. Slow, slow. Control. Confidence. Forget everything except the feel of that cold weapon in my hands.

"Sloan," Elton says, tears streaking his face.

"They won't hurt you," I say simply.

"Animals act on biological impulses," Mr. Foster sputters. "So maybe if—"

"Quiet," I tell him, pulling in a practiced breath.

From the corner of my eye, I see Nash snatch my .22 from Pilot. He doesn't even put the gun into position before he's pulling the trigger. Whatever his target, he misses, but the sound startles the larger female wolf. And the wolf charges Elton.

I line up the shot.

Narrow my eye.

Pull the trigger.

And the animal drops to the ground.

Two of the remaining wolves flee as if they never wanted to be a part of this. They run toward us for a moment, and then veer, heading toward town. Only two stay behind— the black alpha, and the young gray. The male bows his head to the fallen female and whines. When the gray wolf comes to sniff the female too, the male bites at her face and snarls.

The young wolf casts a glance in my direction and holds my stare before dashing after her pack mates. And a moment later, the male leaves too.

Elton crumples to his knees, and Ms. Wade goes to his side.

I move toward the fallen animal. I got it above the back leg, so the animal still kicks. The wolf reaches back to lick the wound, but I can see the creature's insides, and I know it won't live for more than a couple of minutes. I walk over to Nash and yank the .22 from his hands. Then I return to the wolf, and as my stomach rolls, I cock the gun and take aim.

"Don't you dare waste bullets on that thing," Nash says.

I pull a trigger for the second time tonight.

"Idiot!" Nash roars.

But Ms. Wade comes to my defense. "It wouldn't have gone for the boy if you hadn't shot that gun. They were about to scatter when we started yelling."

"What do you know?" Nash says between clenched teeth.

"My husband was our ranger, remember?" Ms. Wade snaps before returning to Elton. "It's okay. They won't come back. They're just looking for food in town because the rabbits are dead. They don't want us."

Elton stands and takes a step toward me. "Thank you."

I shake my head, because killing should never be applauded.

Mr. Foster stares in my direction as if seeing me for the first time. I'm not sure why he's looking at me that way. He knows I'm my father's daughter. He glances at the dead wolf and runs his hands through his hair, shaking his head in shock.

"We're not too far from the first supply shelter," Pilot says.

"We'll be toasting in Vernon by tomorrow night," Nash adds.

"I got some of our things." Mr. Foster mutters, hoisting his pack. "But maybe we should go back for the rest."

No one says anything though. We just stare in the direction we last saw the wolves heading. Toward our town. Toward our homes and warm beds. But those beds won't be warm much longer, and when I glance at Ms. Wade, whose face drips with sweat despite the freezing temperature, I know we don't have a choice.

And so the six of us, together with one terrified basset hound, head into the mouth of the forest in search of the river.

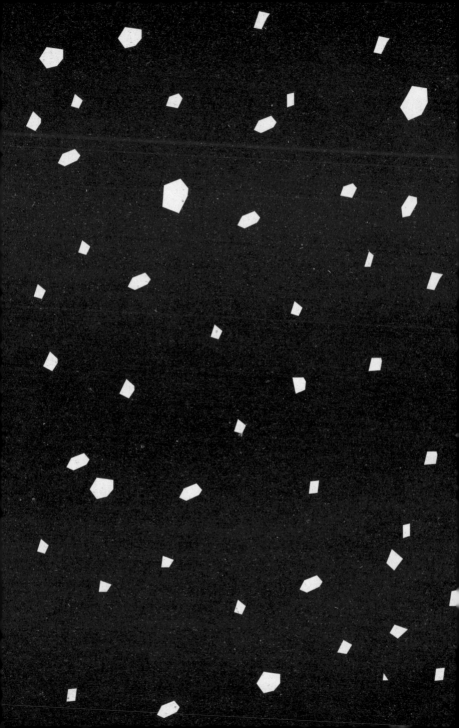

PART II

THE

WOODS

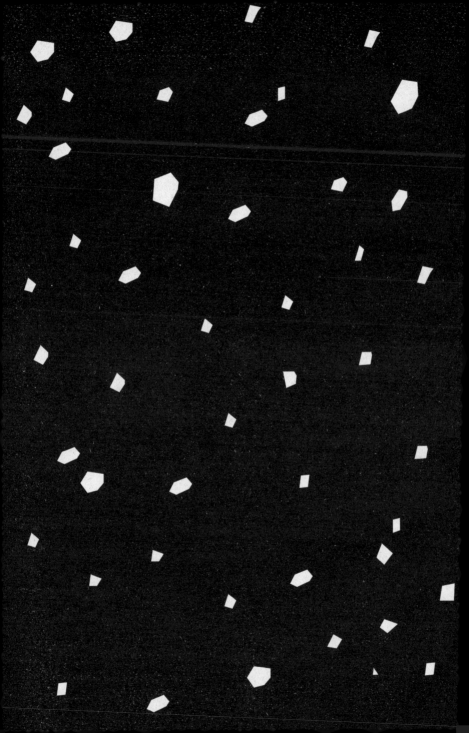

CHAPTER ELEVEN

By the next evening, we are in good spirits, despite the weather. Mr. Foster leads our parade, pointing out plant species and teaching us the names of the stratus clouds overhead—cirro, alto, and nimbo—which sound more like sled dog names to me. Ms. Wade seems revived by walking in the cold air, and Elton is elated to, well, to not have teeth marks. Even Pilot and his father have found common ground, talking at length about the second shelter's location. The first one we passed this morning, stopping only to eat and rest.

Farts romps ahead through the heavy snowfall, barking at squirrels that snub his existence. And as for me? Well, I'm cold. Mr. Foster grabbed our coats before he fled the trailer, which is why he appeared so bulky as he ran. But if I put on every piece of clothing we have between the six of us and wore Farts as a hat, I'd still be shivering.

I wonder how we'll make it through the one, okay, maybe two days it'll take us to arrive at the river when I'm not sure how I'll make it through the hour. And I wonder how much food Mr. Foster has in that pack.

I glance at him, but his eyes are fastened to the ground. Following his gaze, I spot an old animal trap, vintage teeth snapped closed. Inside its mouth are the bones of a deserted animal. Bits of fur are lifted by the wind, and black spots splatter the cruel contraption. I purse my lips, because my father taught me better. We hunt animals for the food they provide, but we don't torture. Pilot catches my eye and shakes his head.

"I'm starving," Elton says, not seeing what we do. His gaze is on the horizon like he can find something to eat without anyone's help. After watching him create that knot in the store, I wonder if he could.

Eyeing Ms. Wade, I say, "Maybe this is a good place to stop."

"The next shelter is close," Pilot says, pointing to three dash marks carved into a tree trunk. Sure enough, after another quarter mile, we come upon the ramshackle structure.

Built of wood planks and a rusted metal roof, the supply shelter stands six feet tall and stretches ten feet across in length and width. We'll be able to sleep inside, the lot of us, but we'll be getting to know each other awfully well.

Mr. Foster glances out the open doorway before sitting. I know why he hesitates. It's the same reason we've covered so much ground since racing into the woods early this morning. When he's satisfied that nothing is following us, he leans against the wall and slides down.

The rest of us find places as I continue to explore our home for the night. The floor is covered in those same wooden planks, and the door is nothing more than a cut of plywood secured by bronze hinges. A stubby stick serves to keep the door closed against the elements, and as Nash steps inside and drops it into place, Mr. Foster pulls off his pack and explores the contents.

"Antibiotic cream," he says, and we nod. "Cheese, more venison, and two sleeves of saltines." Mr. Foster smiles like he's going to play a fun game to ease our minds. "Sloan, if there are eighty crackers here, and we each ate five a day, how long would they last us?"

It's not a hard problem to solve. I know that. But the numbers swirl in my head, even more so with everyone's eyes on me. I see Nash counting on his fingers, his lips moving with his calculations. My blood boils knowing that man will come to a conclusion before I can.

"Not long enough," I mutter.

"How about this instead?" Mr. Foster poses. "Do you know what cloud types we're hoping to see so that we know the blizzard has passed?"

"Who cares?" Pilot interrupts. "It's over when it's over."

The enthusiastic smile on Mr. Foster's face fades. Instead, he gives his head a frustrated shake. "I was just trying to pass the time."

"No, you weren't," I say quietly.

"What's that?"

"I said you weren't trying to pass the time. You were trying to make me feel stupid. You know I can't do math like that in my head. Why don't you ever leave me alone about it?"

Mr. Foster frowns. "I saw the way you shot that wolf, Sloan. If your father pushed education on you half as much as he did hunting you'd be an A student."

I stare at him long and hard until he shrugs.

"You could be a B student," he concedes.

"I knew the answers to your questions," Elton mumbles. "Not that you'd ask me."

Mr. Foster gazes at Elton, confused, but before he can respond, a sound rockets through our small refuge.

The wolves.

They're howling.

Elton pulls his knees to his chest, and stares at the fragile door. We all do. Several tense moments pass—those eerie howls filling the silence—before Ms. Wade begins speaking.

"There aren't as many of them as you may think," she says, her eyes on the boy.

He shrugs like what does he care? But I notice how he

keeps his arms around himself instead of petting that nudging basset hound.

"They each make a unique sound when they howl, and they do it on purpose too. Know why?" she asks.

Elton shakes his head.

It's Nash who leans forward in the dying light. "Why?"

Ms. Wade smiles, amused to have caught the man's interest. "They're showing they're strong in number. Nearly all packs are made up of a breeding male and female, the mother and father, and the pups they bear. Sometimes aunts and uncles and their offspring will stay with the pack too. Just like with humans, those kiddos will eventually leave to form their own families. When they howl like that though, they're trying to sound like a bigger group than they are. The more wolves, the bigger their territory and the stronger they can hold it."

Though I hear their united chorus, it seems to me the wolves aren't simply members of a pack, but are also individuals with personalities and jobs. I've seen females watching over the pups, and alphas showing more bravery than others. But maybe there's one wolf that's the troublemaker, and another that's always playful. And maybe another, like the young gray wolf I've seen, that's the best hunter. I bet wolves have labels too, just like people. And I bet some of them don't like their labels.

Ms. Wade looks back to Elton. "That noise they're making? It's probably the pack warning away others that might be nearby." She beats a closed fist against her chest. "Listen to us. We are strong in number. Find your own territory. Find your own food."

Elton's eyebrows knit together. "What did you mean, a while back, when you said the rabbits are dead?"

The smile leaves Ms. Wade's face. "Well, it's just that . . ."

"We killed them," I answer. "We made more of them, and then we killed 'em."

"Sort of," Ms. Wade answers. "After the tree felling pushed the wolves back, the rabbits lived longer, and so did their offspring. More rabbits had more time to breed. So yes, in the end there were more hares. And that lead to more wolf pups because their food source increased."

"Then we razed the bush," Pilot supplies.

Ms. Wade nods. "Yes, and the rabbits lost their burrows. Then this blizzard came."

Elton leans forward. "So they're all dead? All those rabbits?"

"I would imagine many of them are," Ms. Wade answers.

A worry line forms between his eyes. "So . . . what will the wolves eat now? Now that there are more of them and no rabbits?"

"Caribou," I answer quickly. "Or moose. Or deer."

But Ms. Wade wrings her hands, and I know my response falls flat. Last year my father would come home with a plump caribou once a week. But this year we haven't seen half that number.

"They were building that fence, right?" Mr. Foster says.

"Oh, hush," Ms. Wade clips.

She's trying to protect me because it was my father's idea to build the thing, but I won't be ashamed of him, even if he doesn't deserve my defending him right now.

"Yeah, they built a fence," I say, lifting my chin. "It runs just south of our land, through the woods and to the river, ten or so miles. It's meant to keep the bigger game from leaving after they migrate inland."

"But that's not what happened," Nash says, his voice booming. "The stupid animals went around it, and then it kept them from coming back."

"So the rabbits are gone," Elton says quietly. "And the caribou are gone. And most of the deer and moose too. But the wolves are still here, and there's more of them than ever before."

Nash sits back with a boisterous laugh. "Well, that's fantastic. So we got ourselves a hungry pack of wolves, and we're the only red meat for miles around. And to top it all off, we did this to ourselves!" I grind my teeth as Nash picks at that feeble brain of his. "Well, we'll give them plenty of time to get at us. You can bet your bottoms we ain't making it to Vernon quickly. Not after we dragged our feet through the snow all day."

Nash shoots Ms. Wade an accusatory look. When she opens her mouth to respond, the man cuts her off with a sneer. "Hey, Norma Jean, wasn't that husband of yours reading about the wolves in India before he died? Teddy told Hank that—"

Ms. Wade snaps upright. "Shut your mouth, Nash Blake. You shut it right now or I'll silence you with what strength I have left."

Nash grins and looks at Elton. "Those wolves killed like eighty people, almost all of them kids."

"Nash!"

"Heard Teddy saying one of the kids was taken in front of his own mother, and when the authorities looked for the child later, all they found was the head."

Elton looks at Ms. Wade with fear in his eyes. And I look at Nash with murder in my own. "It's just a story," Elton says with unconvincing confidence. "Right?"

But Ms. Wade only purses her lips and turns away.

The truth lies between us as night invades.

And the wolves continue to howl.

CHAPTER TWELVE

October in Alaska means only ten hours of daylight, which leaves an awful lot of time to lie in the dark and imagine what's lurking outside the shelter walls. But somehow, I find sleep, and when morning comes at last, I wake like an animal, with urges to fill my belly and empty my bladder.

When I see Ms. Wade sleeping against the wall as far away as she can get from Nash, I hesitate. I can't wake her, not when I know she needs the rest. And not when I can make out the dark spot staining the sweater beneath her jacket.

I fidget, knowing I can't go out there alone. Not without someone in sight. But I have to *go*.

It's Pilot who hears me shifting and stands up.

He shuffles for a moment, like he's trying to decide what to say. "I, uh, I gotta go. Will you come with me? Just to be safe?"

I pause, but not for long. After pulling a beanie over his buzzed hair, he pushes open the door. I practically run past him and duck behind a bush. I keep my eyes trained on the boy as I squat, but he never looks in my direction.

The cold gives me an early-morning bare-bottom whopping. And I can tell by looking at the sky that the blizzard isn't ready to release its hold.

As I'm pulling my thermals, jeans, and snow pants back up, I hear the crinkle of that invitation in my pocket. What would it be like if I set aside my fear and accepted? I'll be thirteen in two months' time, and there'd be a chaperone to greet me in Anchorage as soon as I stepped out of that terminal. But I can't even pee alone, so I might as well make a paper airplane out of the invitation and fly it to the moon.

"Hey, Sloan," Pilot says when I appear from the bush, my stomach growling, the relentless snow nipping at my cheeks. "I wanted to talk with you about . . . about your dad and sister."

I stride toward our shelter as my face heats. "Let's not and say we did."

Pilot takes hold of my arm, and I stop. "They caught a ride with my mom, did you know that? When I didn't see you with them . . . I wouldn't have left you, all right? That's all I'm getting at."

"Don't you dare act like you stayed behind for me," I bark. And then, lowering my voice, I add, "I'd hate myself if you did."

"I stayed because I thought my dad would be there. I told you as much." He shrugs with a slight smile. "And I stayed because you gave me gloves once upon a time."

"That wasn't me," I say.

Pilot laughs. "Yeah, it was."

"You never wore them."

"Because I was embarrassed you noticed." Pilot releases my arm and glances away, like whatever he has to say next will sting coming out. "I know what it's like to have a parent disappoint you, okay?"

I look up at Pilot. Realize how much taller he is than me. And almost two years older. I bet he's kissed half a dozen girls. Pilot may not have many friends, but his face could convince any girl to lean closer. Does he know that?

"Okay," is all I say before heading back, listening hard so I can be sure he's close behind. I hate that we have this unfortunate thing in common, and that he may understand me better than most. But I'm also frustrated that I'm thin and awkward and undeveloped in my older sister's curvy shadow. He must think I'm so childish.

I shake the thought from my head as Mr. Foster appears from the shelter.

"We should get started early," he says with a yawn. "Maybe we can get to the river today if we travel fast enough."

Pilot walks past, throwing Mr. Foster a nod. Before he heads inside, Pilot glances back with a look I'd like to bottle. Maybe he *doesn't* look at me like a child. Maybe he doesn't look at me that way at all.

Silently, I throw my lasso around Pilot's waist.

Pilot says there are four more shelters between here and the river. As we follow him to the next one, I huddle against the wind and snow, which rages meaner than ever. I try to recognize something in my surroundings, though I can hardly see through the whirling white. I spot a seventy-foot paper birch and an enormous boulder my mother and I may have passed on our way to the river two years ago. But I'd followed my mother blindly that day, a planet orbiting the sun out of some gravitational pull. My eyes had been on my feet, and on her, and on the bag of spiced peanuts she'd brought for the walk.

Ms. Wade holds tight to my arm as we travel. I like the sensation, the weight of her fingers reminding me I'm not alone. Even without my father and sister, I can stand upright. I just need someone else to lean on. Is that so wrong?

She's moving slower today, but then we barely ate this

morning, trying to ration what food remains. As Pilot carries my .22, I silently count those bullets over and over— four for my father's rifle, and four for my own. Ms. Wade stumbles and I glance over at her, at those soft blue eyes set in the folds of her face and the hard lines on either side of her mouth. I rarely see her smile, but I know her insides are good. She's a strong woman, and that's more important than wearing a pretty smile for the world's sake.

Ms. Wade's color is pink. Pink like a blush. Pink like the flat of my tongue. A pink you can trust through and through even if it wants people to think otherwise. Ms. Wade probably thinks her color is a little red, like Nash's. But it's not.

"I keep thinking about things," Ms. Wade says when the others are out of earshot.

"What sorts of things?"

"Teddy, mostly. How I wish he were here. He wasn't the cuddle-up type, but he always held me as I fell asleep. Sometimes it's not what we do of our own accord, but what we do despite it going against our nature." She nods. "That's how you love."

I'm not sure if that's right or not, but because I think it's good to keep her talking, I ask, "Do you hear from your boys often?"

"Occasionally. I call them from the store when I can. They've got little ones of their own now, you know—Cliff just had a son, and David has two girls, just like your daddy does. I'm going to see them one of these days." She hesitates, and then says with certainty, "This coming spring."

Ms. Wade looks at me from the corner of her eye. "I remember when my boys were still babies. I always wanted them to need me more than they did. David walked by the time he was ten months old 'cause he saw his older brother doing it. But Cliff took longer. He did this thing they call cruising. It's where a toddler holds on to furniture as they move about the house. They can walk fine on their own, mind you. But they're too afraid to let go. They don't trust themselves." Ms. Wade pauses. "You hear what I'm telling you?"

I shrug, because I'm not sure I do.

"Your mama wasn't happy, Sloan," Ms. Wade says suddenly, firmly. "And there was nothing anyone could have done to make it so."

I stop walking, stunned silent.

Ms. Wade takes my chin in her hand and forces me to look in her eyes. "I know your daddy left you so that you might be more independent. But it's okay to hold tight to people. If you don't want to be alone after your mama left and you got lost in those woods, then I say so what. But you got to know her going wasn't your fault. When she took off in search of another life, it was for herself, understand?"

My eyes dart away, staring at the same woods I raced into after I found my mother's note. I was sure if I found Mama's ruby ring, she'd come back.

Maybe Ms. Wade is right. Maybe it wasn't my fault she left. But if I'd have seen her color—blue, blue, blue like storm clouds and the veins on the inside of your wrists—I would have known that she would leave.

I would have known what to expect.

"Look at me, Sloan," Ms. Wade says. "You're okay."

Something inside me threatens to break free, like holding tight to a balloon, but wanting to watch it float toward the sky too.

Her words are buried by the sound of Pilot yelling. Nash has his arms locked around his son, and he wrestles him forward. Ms. Wade releases me, and I fly toward my lifeline.

I'm twenty paces away when I spot the steep ledge.

CHAPTER THIRTEEN

Nash pushes his son closer to the ravine, the blizzard making it hard to see how near they are to the ledge. Mr. Foster grabs at Nash's shoulders, but the man moves out of reach. Soon, Nash is too near the edge to risk doing anything. If we startle Nash, he could release his son and send him tumbling to his death. Pilot's face is frozen with horror, my childhood rifle forgotten in the snow. His toes skim the ground, and when he flails, I watch those boots leave the ground in favor of open space.

Nash locks his son against his chest for a moment, and then a slow smile parts his mouth. A laugh breaks across the forest as Nash steps back and thrusts Pilot away from the drop.

"Just about wet yourself again, boy!" Nash holds his stomach and laughs. "That's what you get for not trusting your old man."

I half expect Pilot to charge him, but he only grips the

snow, seeking the earth beneath his fingers, trying to reassure himself that he's safe on solid ground.

Mr. Foster grabs Nash by his jacket and jerks him so that their noses touch. "Lay one more finger on your kid. I dare you."

"Oh, ho, ho!" Nash chuckles. "What's a big man like you gonna do?"

He's taunting Mr. Foster, thinking he won't do a thing. But I don't forget the ledge behind both men. I don't dismiss the damage two angry hands could do with one shove.

I reach down to help Pilot up, but he scrambles to his feet on his own. Together, Pilot and I watch Mr. Foster to see what our teacher may do under pressure.

With a jolt, Mr. Foster releases Nash. Then he holds up a stiff finger and points it at Nash's face in a silent warning. For once, Pilot's daddy keeps his mouth shut, but he can't manage it without an infuriating grin.

Nash reaches for his son and rubs his knuckles into his hair. "You know I was playing, right? I used to do that kind of stuff all the time. Always made you laugh before."

Pilot swats his father's hand. "It never made me laugh."

"Yeah, well, that's because you have your mama's sense of humor. Which is to say you're both dry as a turd on a summer day."

As Nash laughs, I notice the way his left hand shakes at his side. He's twitchier than usual, if that's possible.

Ms. Wade approaches the ledge, keeping a wary eye on Nash. "Looks like a good twenty feet."

"We'll have to go around somehow," I add.

"Can't," Nash says. "This stretches on too far. We'll just climb down and keep going."

I look at Nash. How can he be sure? I don't remember this ravine. Does he? A horrible thought occurs to me amid the howling wind. *What if we're lost?*

"What about Farts?" Elton asks.

"Oh, I'll carry the stupid thing," Nash responds. "Put him in the pack and zip it up so his head sticks out."

I'm surprised at Nash's offer, but then no one is completely rotten, even if it seems that way. We've all got a little good, and a little ugly. Some just have more of one than the other. Nash looks at his son to see if the suggestion helped make amends, but Pilot only hands the pack's contents to Mr. Foster to store in his pockets. Then he slides the dog and the pack onto his own back with a mighty grunt. Good thing Farts is still mostly a puppy, or there's no way he'd manage.

Now that that's settled, we look at Ms. Wade.

"Oh, get off it," she says. "I could climb down this thing three times over again before any one of you buffoons could." To prove her point, Ms. Wade makes her way to the side. "Plenty of footholds. Just make a slow go of it."

"I'll try first," I say, grabbing Ms. Wade's arm. "I can find the best way down."

But Elton is already swinging his leg over the side.

I scowl. Did he not hear me?

I hold my breath as Elton navigates the rock wall. He moves quickly and efficiently, finding a foothold, testing it, and dropping down. Before I know it, Elton has made it to the bottom. I frown, because his color is yellow like mine, which means he shouldn't have been the first down. He should have been more cautious. Wanted to watch and wait even if he pretended otherwise.

"I'll go next," Pilot says, getting into position. Farts barks the entire time the boy navigates down, increasing the anxiety twisting my insides. I watch every move Pilot makes, hoping the snow will suddenly stop, calculating how badly he'd be hurt with each step.

Twenty feet high—a broken leg, maybe worse.

Fifteen feet—a sprained ankle to be sure.

Ten feet—he's in the clear, I think.

Ms. Wade looks to me after Pilot is on safe ground. "You gonna insist on going before or after me?"

Sucking in a breath, I slide toward the edge on my

belly and squirm backward until my bottom half hangs over the side.

I don't want to go any farther.

I can't.

But Ms. Wade is watching. How much harder will it be for her to do this if she watches me struggle?

My hands begin to sweat. How is that possible when they're so numb I can hardly feel them? My gloves dangle from inside my pocket as I work my fingers into the first rock crevice, unable to focus with snow rushing past my eyes. The stones are slick from the blizzard, so I dig my nails in until they bend backward.

How did Elton and Pilot do this? Why am I having trouble when they didn't?

I bite my lip, and my arms shake as I take one miniscule step down. Pilot must notice I'm struggling, because he calls out.

"You got it, Sloan! Just go slow."

His concern causes fear to snake around my wrists and ankles. If he's worried enough to say something, then I must be about to fall.

My vision blurs. My brain buzzes.

I take another step—

And I lose my grip.

I scream, and feel myself falling. Hear the sound of my

leg bones snapping in my mind. But at the last possible second, I find my grip on a larger rock. I'm still breathless and can't see more than six inches in front of my eyes. I'm frozen with fear. Can't go up, can't go down, and it's just a matter of time until I fall for real.

"For goodness' sake, girl," Ms. Wade calls out. "You're not that high up. Move that rear or I'm going to start throwing rocks at you."

Farts barks from below and Nash bellows somewhere above me and just like that, a sliver of my terror dissolves.

I stretch my leg downward and find a new place to squeeze in the tip of my boot. Summoning every ounce of courage I have, I release the rock I'm gripping and search for a new, lower hold. I do this again, and again, and again, and when at last I've reached the ground, and Pilot slaps me on the back and Elton says I climb like a girl, I beam with satisfaction.

Because this was a fear I didn't even know I had. And I overcame it. Not one other person was on that cliff face but me. And I did it anyway.

I pick up Farts and kiss him on his wet nose. He thanks me kindly by windshield-wiping my face with his tongue.

Ms. Wade climbs down next, and though I hear her moaning the entire way, she completes the descent twice as fast as either of the boys. After she steps onto the ground, she leans over and grips her side.

"Are you okay?" I ask. "Ms. Wade, how bad does it hurt?"

Her reply comes in the form of fresh droplets of blood, red starbursts staining the white quilt of snow. She straightens after another moment, and assures us she's fine. Tells me to quit fussing.

The next thing I hear is the ruckus of Nash and Mr. Foster arguing. Voices raised, a scattering of rocks tumbles down the ravine. We all look up, and I catch sight of Mr. Foster as he nears the edge.

My stomach plummets.

CHAPTER FOURTEEN

My hand is already in the first hole when Pilot yanks me backward. "The guns are up there with them," I yell. "I left them!" But now Ms. Wade is helping drive me away, saying it's no one person's responsibility to watch over those rifles.

I struggle against Pilot until the two men's bickering becomes a mighty roar. There's a rustling sound, and a moment later I see Mr. Foster appear. He throws my mag off the side of the cliff and it lands with a soft whump in the snow. Farts barks at the thing like it's got sharp teeth and a hankering for basset hound blood.

I'd be relieved, but my daddy's gun is still up there—the one that could put a hole through a bear's gut and keep on going.

When I look up again, I see Nash scurrying toward the side. He's on his stomach and that beautiful heirloom rifle is jammed down the back of his pants. Mr. Foster makes a play for it, but Nash slaps his hand and nearly tumbles twenty feet down in the process. Mr. Foster swings his arms wildly, trying to keep his own feet on solid ground, and Nash makes for the earth below.

"I know what you were trying to do," Mr. Foster yells at Nash.

Nash grunts as he climbs, but still manages to retort with, "I wasn't doing nothing. Just trying to get the guns down is all."

As soon as Nash is within arm's length, I snatch my father's rifle. Nash snaps at my fingers as he jumps the rest of the way down. But Ms. Wade has my back, and my gun.

"You'll step away if you know what's good for you," she says to Nash. "What were you doing to him up there?"

Nash ignores her and looks to his son. "Nothing he didn't deserve."

"No," Pilot says between clenched teeth. "You'd never do anything to anyone who didn't deserve it."

"Now, now, you're trying to challenge me. And you know I don't like being disrespected."

Pilot opens his mouth to add more, but it's Elton who speaks next.

"Why isn't Mr. Foster coming down?"

Almost at once, we stop what we're doing—cradling a rifle to our chest or confronting a nasty father or fingering a wound that'd be better left alone—and we gaze skyward.

"Mr. Foster?" Elton calls out.

When the man doesn't appear, and not a single sound makes its way down the ravine, our eyes slowly move to Nash.

"What did you do?" I ask.

"Oh, lay off it. I didn't put a finger on the man. He was too busy clawing at my face like a dang woman for me to get a lick in."

"If you hurt him . . ." Pilot threatens, his voice low.

"He's still up there," Ms. Wade says. "I hear his boots in the snow."

We listen.

We listen *hard*.

And that's when I hear it too—quick steps. Alert steps. A low whine and a quick yelp and a growl that rumbles down the cliff and beneath my skin.

The sound of wolves.

CHAPTER FIFTEEN

I grab my father's gun, tuck it under my arm, and throw myself toward the rocks. Pilot has his arms around me in a flash. "I'll go! Stay put," he says. I scramble toward the cliff again, and again Pilot pulls me back. "Just make noise, Sloan! Do it now!"

As the whines and growls grow in volume, and desperation boils through my veins, I yell and cry and shout ugly words. Elton and Ms. Wade and even Nash join me. We sound like madmen. We sound like animals. As Pilot climbs into the sky, we harmonize, offering our own howls to the dawning winter moon.

Mr. Foster releases a cry of pain. Or at least I think it's pain. I can't make out what's what amid the chorus of wolf and man colliding. Pilot is only halfway up the cliff when I remember our advantage.

I grab my .22 mag from Ms. Wade and take aim at the clouds. A shot rings through the dusk, but the growls only increase. Tossing my gun, I take my father's rifle and prepare to chase the first shot with a second. Nash yanks my elbow, causing me to nearly shoot his son in the process.

"What are you doing?" Nash hisses. "Don't waste bullets unless it's to kill those things."

I grit my teeth and jerk away. Point that barrel toward heaven and send a bullet blasting through the clouds.

This time, something happens. There's a yelp from above, and a patter of receding steps. Then one ferocious growl, a snap of teeth, and at last I see Mr. Foster.

He spins toward us, his face contorted with terror.

Then he falls.

He falls for twenty feet and crashes into the snow with a terrible crunch.

Elton is the first to his side. "Mr. Foster! Mr. Foster, are you all right?" He touches the man's exposed cheek gently with slim, shaking fingers. When Mr. Foster doesn't move, Elton lays a hand on the man's back and closes his eyes in concentration.

At last, the boy lifts his head. "He's breathing."

Mr. Foster stirs ever so slightly. "Course I am."

Ms. Wade laughs with relief as Nash says, "I coulda shoved you off that cliff a lot more graceful than that, man."

Mr. Foster rolls onto his side with a groan, takes several slow, calming breaths, and finally sits up.

"Does anything hurt?" Pilot asks.

Mr. Foster rolls his neck and releases a groan. "I think the pinkie toe on my right foot made it through okay."

I help Mr. Foster to his feet, and he staggers before finding his balance. "The snow cushioned some of the impact."

"Well, dang," Nash says. "Guess we all coulda just lunged off the side. Would have saved a bit of time."

Elton looks toward the cliff and asks, "Those were wolves up there, huh?"

Mr. Foster grows serious. "Yeah. I counted six."

"You didn't . . ." Elton begins. "You didn't get bit, did you?"

"I'm not sure," Mr. Foster says. "But I suddenly have an insatiable craving for red meat."

Elton's eyes grow large. "You think you're gonna turn into one of them?"

"Undoubtedly."

"Stop kidding around. We need to get out of here." Pilot picks up my .22 and motions toward the trees with the barrel. "It's almost dark, and this blizzard's going to kill us if we don't get to the next shelter."

Elton gazes at the cliff again, shielding his eyes against the snow. "Maybe it's good. Maybe the wolves won't be able to come down like we did."

We don't respond. We just march toward those trees,

toward the river, raising our knees higher to pass through the deepening powder. Mr. Foster stumbles several times as he walks, but what worries me is the way he holds his arm close to his body. If it's a broken bone, he could get an infection. Happens to people in town who break something and put off traveling to Vernon's doctor.

But despite his fall and Ms. Wade's heavy breathing, I feel a sense of relief as we move farther from the cliff. Maybe Elton is right. Maybe the wolves won't find a path down, and our only hurdle now is the weather and those few miles that stand between Mr. Clive's boat and us. We figured we'd be in Vernon tonight, but surely now that we're down the cliff we'll be there tomorrow.

My mouth waters thinking of the honey-glazed chicken and roasted corn I'll eat beside a roaring fire, and the sleep I'll get on Edna's couch, with a crochet blanket pulled to my shoulders and the sound of my father talking with Edna's husband close by.

"Is that what I think it is?" Elton asks after we've walked for some time.

We stop and look back. A chill races across my skin, makes my fingertips tingle. In the distance, atop the cliff, is the silhouette of nine wolves. Maybe Mr. Foster counted wrong, or maybe the other three didn't show themselves. How many more could there be?

The wolves watch us watching them, and a memory springs to mind. I recall the two wolves chasing the snowshoe hare across the field. How fast they claimed that animal as their prize. I remember wondering how the rabbit's heart must have raced. How it must have known without doubt that it would be eaten.

I think about this as we turn our backs on the wolves, and head deeper into the woods. I try to bury the worry, because we're not rabbits. We are humans. We are *hunters*.

We are not prey.

CHAPTER SIXTEEN

Ms. Wade can no longer pretend that she is well enough to travel far distances. The smell from her wound makes the back of my throat tighten, and when Mr. Foster removes her bandage and rubs the open wound with snow, she weeps from the pain.

We've been out in the cold for two full days, and though the blizzard has eased, snow still dusts the rooftop of our rickety shelter. So we watch each other's Rudolph-red noses, and wait for night to pass.

When Nash's stomach protests, the man says again—two hours into us dozing and shifting, shifting and dozing—that Mr. Foster should never have thrown the venison and cheese at the wolves. That now we have nothing but an empty pack to get us to the river.

"I suppose you'd rather I'd offered my fingers," Mr. Foster growls through a sleepy haze, losing his patience in this blistering cold.

"What need do I have for your fingers?" Nash says.

"Maybe if you hadn't been fighting me for the guns like a gorilla," Mr. Foster retorts, sitting up, "the wolves wouldn't have come at all."

I do my best to ignore the conversation, and instead thumb the slip of paper in my pocket back and forth. I'm certain nobody notices, but then Elton bites his lip and says, "Why do you always do that? Put that hand in your pocket?"

I pull my fingers out, mortified.

"Leave her alone, Elton Von . . . Whatever." Pilot rolls onto his side, face scrunching in thought. "Why'd you choose that strange name anyway?"

Mr. Foster and Nash stop their complaining and turn their attention to us. Because even though people in Rusic try to keep their personal lives private, our town thrives on gossip.

"Let's go back to the note in your pocket," Elton says. But even Ms. Wade is paying attention now, pulling herself up as best she can.

"Let's not," Pilot says with a smile.

Elton sighs, realizing we're not going to let it go, and enjoying that he has a captive audience. It must feel good to have people pay attention to you after being ignored for so long. "Christopher Anders is a ridiculous name."

"Why?" Mr. Foster asks.

Elton rolls his eyes. "It just is. Christopher Anders is someone my mom wants me to be. But I'm different, and thank goodness for that." He says this with a determined look. "So I gave myself a new name, based on people I like." He counts off on his fingers. "Elton John is a musician to end all musicians. And Dean for James Dean, a true rebel."

"What about the *Von* part?" Pilot asks.

Elton shrugs. "You can't have a name like Elton Dean without throwing in *Von* for good measure."

Pilot and I laugh, and Mr. Foster bumps Elton's shoulder.

"It's a fine name," he says.

Elton grins. "The fact that you realize that means you *might* be okay. And the fact that you almost got eaten by wolves means you're a legend."

Mr. Foster smiles while clutching his arm, recalling his fall.

"Your turn now," Nash says, studying me. "All of Rusic has been watching you walk around with that stupid paper for the better part of a year. So go on, what is it?"

"You don't have to tell him," Pilot says.

"Oh, yes she does." Elton grins. "A secret for a secret. That's the deal."

"I didn't ask about your name," I mumble. But the longer everyone waits, the bolder I become. Maybe it's the warmth from our bodies after being so cold. Or maybe it's boredom. Or maybe it's because we've been in this shelter for three hours, and everyone's colors blend together so brightly it causes my brain to ache.

"I got invited to the Junior Art Competition in Anchorage. Someone sent in photos of my work, I guess, and they thought it was good enough for me to come out."

"When is it?" Pilot asks.

I swallow. "March."

"Don't they give like millions of dollars to the winner?" Elton says.

"Not sure it's quite that much," Mr. Foster says. "But it's probably a good bit of money. If you won, you could use it for proper schooling when you get older. Go to college. You could get accepted as an art major, and then transfer to something else once you got in. Maybe agricultural science or rangeland ecology."

"Or you could buy all your friends a satellite TV," Elton supplies with a grin. "That's what a good friend would do." Elton says the word *friend* like he's afraid I'll bite him.

"Your daddy gonna go with you?" Ms. Wade asks softly.

I shake my head. "Nah, we don't have the money for that. I got a scholarship for the flight, and they said I could stay with this woman volunteer for a night." I look at Mr. Foster. "She's like you. A teacher."

"We're all the same," he says with a wink.

"So you'll go," Elton says firmly.

My silence says everything.

"You too chicken to go alone?" Nash says. "Because of getting lost in the woods?"

I bite my lip and turn away, and no matter how hard I fight it—*Don't you do it! Don't you dare do it!*—I feel a burning at the back of my eyes. Not because the memory upsets me that much, but because it's mortifying when every last person knows your shame.

"It's time to get over that, if you ask me," Nash says, leaning back on his elbows. "Wise of your pop to leave you behind. You need to grow up. So you spent a few days alone out there. So what?"

In that moment, three things happen—

Mr. Foster pulls his arm back to bust Nash's nose.

Pilot lunges across the shelter like he's going to take that honor himself.

And I beat them both to the punch and throw my fist into Nash Blake's teeth.

His head snaps back with a satisfying pop, but I'm not done with him yet. I'm tired of the way he treats everyone in our group. I don't care that he hasn't visited a bar in days, or how he came to be the way he is. I only care that he's a bully.

"I may be a coward," I tell him. "But you're spoiled on the inside. You're rotten, and you don't deserve a son like Pilot. You deserve to be all alone!"

Nash fingers a bit of blood from inside his cheek. "Did I just get hit by a twelve-year-old girl?" He laughs, and the sound makes me furious. "Felt like a swat from a kitten."

His words burrow into my brain, but I also see how Pilot is biting back laughter. And then suddenly, he's not. Pilot roars, rolling onto his opposite side and gripping his stomach as he hoots. Elton joins him, and even Mr. Foster laughs.

"You should have seen your face," Pilot says to his father, barely able to get the words out. He imitates his dad's surprised face, and then breaks into another round of body-shaking laughter.

Ms. Wade smiles, bringing color to her cheeks. Even me—I start to smile too. Nash chuckles like he's in on the joke. And Pilot's basset hound jumps with excitement at the sound. And then the dog, he . . .

The worst smell I have ever smelled in my entire life wheezes through our shelter. We stop laughing and howl in disgust.

One by one we zip from the shelter and into the open air, away from that horrible stink. Away from a dog named Farts who loves the taste of cabbage and can clear a room in a matter of seconds.

"I'll never breathe through my nose again!" Elton screams with half disgust, half delight.

"I've smelled skunk spray before," Mr. Foster says. "But that dog could stink a skunk to high heaven."

"Might as well keep moving since we're out here," Ms. Wade adds. "I'm not sleeping inside that thing now."

"You wanna walk in the dark?" Elton asks, his laughter fading.

I'm thinking the same thing, but when I see the concerned press of Ms. Wade's lips, I say to her, "It'll be harder going at night."

Indecision twists her face as we war against moving now for her sake, and sticking with the shelter's warmth for our own. Finally, she says, "I've got to move when I have the strength. And right now I'm invigorated by that dog."

"Well, someone's got to go back in and get the guns at least." Pilot scratches at his wind-chapped cheek, knowing that person will be him. And when no one offers to do the job, he sucks in a deep breath and rushes inside. He reappears seconds later, cheeks puffed out, two guns held under his arm, and a basset hound gripped between his hands—rear end facing out.

"Oh!" we all yell as he nears us.

"You know where we're headed?" Mr. Foster asks Pilot.

"Him?" Nash interrupts. "That boy would lose his own head if weren't attached to his body. He's fooled you if you think it's him who found the first three shelters. *I'm* the one who knows the way to the river." The man smiles at me until my skin crawls. "Pity to think what would happen without good ol' Nash around."

"We'd manage," I say as nerves knot my insides, because, yeah, I did think Pilot knew where we were headed.

"I've made the trip once," Pilot mutters.

I think about adding that I've made the same trip myself, but I don't want to talk about my mom, or share the other reason I'm longing to see the river.

"Enough chitchat," Ms. Wade says, stepping between Nash and me. "You two have just about worn me out." Then she adds, much quieter, "Is everyone okay with this? We don't have to—"

"We can do it," Mr. Foster says.

Pilot and I nod, and eventually, Elton does too.

Nash continues to glare at me, his upper lip pulled away from his teeth. Then he bends over, spits into the snow, and takes the lead.

Before I follow him, I notice there's a bit of blood mixed

with his saliva. I don't feel bad about hitting Nash. I know I didn't hurt him much, but I popped him good enough to draw blood. My father may not be the best there is, but he's a better sort than Nash Blake. And I know without a shadow of a doubt that if he saw me take a fist to that man's mouth, well, that'd make my daddy smile something fierce.

CHAPTER SEVENTEEN

We've been walking for hours—much too far to retrace our steps—when we realize we're lost. It's dark in the forest this late at night. The kind of dark that seeps into your ears and taps on your brain. It whispers in the quiet as you crunch through the snow.

I am here, behind the trees.

I grow closer though you cannot hear.

Did you feel that? I just brushed your cheek.

I spin around, heart pounding, searching for whatever I felt. But there's nothing there but dead leaves clinging to branches. They take on the shapes of yellow claws and hungry jaws and monsters with bottomless bellies.

"We're going to have to stop and rest," Mr. Foster says, rubbing that aching arm of his.

"What, *here*?" Elton asks.

"I know I can find it," Nash growls. "Stupid woman must have moved it or something."

"We'll freeze." Elton crouches down to pet the basset hound, and that dog is all too happy to bury his head into the boy's chest. "We have to keep looking. Right?"

Even in the dark, I can see how Ms. Wade hunches over, gloved hands on her knees. I'd hoped we would make it to the river tomorrow. If we'd waited until daylight, when Nash could see better, maybe we would have. But now we're off whatever path he remembers, and who knows how long it'll take to find our way. I gaze skyward, and notice the snowfall has slowed. Even the wind seems to have slowed. We'd celebrate if we weren't facing a night spent outside, exposed.

When I drop into the snow, and Pilot does the same, Elton sighs. "Okay. Okay, I can help." The boy disappears into the forest even as I yell for him to return. Pilot yells too, mostly for Elton to bring back his dog. Elton reappears a few moments later with an armful of dried bark and leaves, Farts yapping at his heels.

Elton drops the kindling and rocks he collected, then waves his arms toward the snow. "Clear it down to the dirt, then cover it with dry clothing."

Realizing what he's aiming at, Pilot jumps to attention. He cups his hands and rakes away the snow. Then he opens his jacket and, before anyone can object, pulls off his sweater, long-sleeved thermal shirt, and finally, the thin long-sleeved shirt beneath that.

I can't drag my eyes away from Pilot's bare chest, though my face reddens at the sight of him partially undressed. When Ms. Wade sees me staring, I turn away, embarrassed.

"Pilot, you'll get hypothermia," Mr. Foster says. But he doesn't offer to spare any of his own clothing.

"It's just a shirt." Pilot lays the cloth over the ground, and Elton puts the dry twigs he foraged on top as Pilot re-dresses. Then he begins cutting the rocks against each other. The sound echoes through the clearing, and I can't help wondering what animals it might attract.

"I can do that," Nash says, moving closer. "Here, I'm stronger."

"No, there's an art to it." Elton keeps striking the rocks. "Well, that and some patience. Pilot, hold your jacket around my hands so the wind doesn't steal my spark."

It must take Elton two hundred false starts before those crispy leaves start to singe. Elton bends low and cups his hands around them, blowing gently. "Grab the bark chips. Dry them in your gloves and then rub them between your bare hands. Quick!"

Pilot does as he says, snatching up the dead bark, and I jump in to help. When I tear the gloves from my hands, I gasp from the cold.

Before long, a humble fire springs to life. Elton leaps back and gives the fire room to breathe.

We dive forward, warming our hands, whooping with joy at this small miracle.

Mr. Foster rubs his hands before the flame and looks at Elton with wonder. "That was fantastic. A shining example of science at work. You're a bright kid, Elton Dean Von Anders."

"It's not science; it's survival," I say. "There's a difference." I look from Mr. Foster to Elton and add, "But either way, it was wicked cool."

Elton beams, and I scoot closer to him. Bump his shoulder with my own as something passes between us. *The makings of a friendship,* my heart says hopefully. *From someone who understands what you've been through.*

"We need dead branches," Elton says, snapping back into survival mode. "We can dry them over the fire and use them as torches. The fire won't stay on the ground long."

"How'd you learn to do this?" Nash asks.

Elton shrugs. "My brother wanted to be a marine before he decided on college. Said you had to know how to survive in enemy territory as a soldier. After he left, I read all his books." Elton glances at the rocks he cast aside. "Those are quartz. Not too hard to find near water. We must be getting close to the river."

His words ignite hope in my chest. It remains there as we light the torches. As we settle our backs against tree trunks and decide on watch shifts.

"We should watch in pairs until the sun rises," I suggest. "I can go first if someone wants to partner with me."

"I can go with you," Elton says.

I smile.

I move close to Elton as silence settles over bent heads, blistered mouths buried into scarves. The others fall into a restless sleep as I work to find a way to talk with Elton.

Eventually, I decide to simply say my thoughts outright. "Must have been hard when your brother left, huh?"

Elton's eyes snap to mine, cautious.

There's that yellow.

Elton crosses his legs. Rubs his hands over his knees. "He was my best friend." The boy releases a long, tired breath. "He was my only friend, I guess. He took care of me."

"You have your mom though, right?" I ask gently.

"As much as you do."

His comparison stings, but I find myself nodding. "She that bad?"

Elton smiles, but it isn't a happy smile. "It's like she only had enough love for one kid, and there's no way I was winning that contest. She's mad he left, which makes it worse." Elton frowns, and I can tell he's fighting pain as big as my own. "I'm mad he left too. He knew how she was to me. He *knew*."

I try to puzzle out how to make Elton feel better. In the

end, I say, "I think . . . I think it's hard to see ourselves different than how our parents see us. I didn't know your brother, but you seem pretty cool to me."

Elton squints and looks away like he's trying to find something in the distance. After a quiet moment, he glances at me and says, "Well, I think you're really brave, and smart too."

Intuitive and vulnerable.

I grin. "When this is all over, maybe we should hang out. I could show you how to hunt squirrels."

Elton nods, eyes dancing. "And I could show you how to spit-fish. It's a way of fishing using only your shirt and the saliva in your mouth!"

I have to press my lips together to keep from laughing. "Sounds good to me."

Elton looks at a sleeping Pilot. "Maybe we should let him hang out with us too. I like his dog."

My eyes fall on Pilot, on the angles of his face, both hard and soft at once. "That'd be okay, I guess." I grin at Elton. "Then there'd be three of us. We could make a lot of trouble."

"We'll drive Mr. Foster crazy," Elton says through a giggle.

"Excellent."

I stare up at the trees, and Elton does the same. After a long while, the boy says with a sigh, "I miss him so much."

I bite my lip. "He'll be back, Elton."

He nods, head still tilted upward. Then he asks, in that quiet voice I've learned to like, "Do you think your mom will come back?"

I bite down as tears sting my eyes. "No," I say softly. "No, she won't come back."

Despite struggling to keep his eyes open, Elton falls asleep. Without our conversation, the forest grows quiet. What happened to the hooting of those great horned owls? What happened to the black spruce trees that moaned under the weight of winter?

The silence is terrifying. Not because I'm afraid of what lies beneath it, but because it offers my mind room to spin.

CHAPTER EiGHTEEN

Pilot wakes up, shivering so hard it looks as if he's shaking his head no. If I were the girl I was before I got lost in the woods, maybe I'd hold his hand and say that I was only ever angry with him because he reminds me of what a coward I am. Because out there all alone, with my left ear pressed into the snow, I was empty. I wasn't afraid. I wasn't angry. I was just *done*.

I'd spent the first three days searching for town, humiliated that I ever believed I could find the river on my own. Or that my mother would return if I did.

It was the fifth day that I gave up.

When I first heard Pilot's voice it sounded so distant I was terrified he'd slip away. But I didn't move. Even as hope burst through every cell in my body. I lay there, numb and dumb and crying so hard my body shook as Pilot's does now.

I wanted him to find me.

And I didn't.

Pilot scoots toward me. When I don't say anything, he takes it as an invitation and moves so that we're side by side, my good ear facing his cheek. Our arms press together, and he begins to calm. But after only a few minutes of silence, a noise startles me. It's a light crunching sound. A shuffling between bushes. The hair on my arms rises.

"Did you hear that?" I ask Pilot.

He nods.

We hold our breath and my scalp tingles, waiting to see what made that sound. It comes again, faster. The sound of light footsteps. Of webbed paws.

I see them before Pilot does.

Those eyes.

Those eyes staring at us from behind a wall of darkness. There are no growls or barks or excited yips. Wolves are not dogs. They are quiet, patient. They creep silently—noses low—upon their prey. Just as they have done to us now.

Pilot races toward a set of eyes and swings our torch in their direction. "Get back! Get out of here!"

Almost immediately, the rest of our camp is on their feet. Elton screams and Mr. Foster nearly falls into the fire and Nash demands to know why everyone is carrying on. I've got my father's gun poised before another word can leave another mouth.

Three bullets left in this gun.

Three in the other.

Is it worth it?

Yes.

Pilot swings the torch, yelling and stomping his feet. The wolves back away, but they don't flee. We're too exposed out here. The smell of blood on Ms. Wade is too strong. I take aim at the closest pair of eyes, and step toward them.

I breathe in. Breathe out.

Fire.

I missed! I can't believe it. The eyes dashed out of view the moment before that third-to-last bullet whizzed from my father's gun. Doesn't matter. Those yellow eyes wink out, two at a time, until none remain. No one speaks for a long time. We turn in nervous circles, breathing hard, waiting for a wolf to lunge, though it goes against anything we've ever known about them.

But I know them in a different way than the others, don't I? Ms. Wade may know their behavior, and their culture, but I know a hunter's mind—the way it locks on its prey and doesn't let go. They have us in their sights, in their noses, and they'll choose one of two paths in the future. They'll hide among the trees and creep silently upon us as they did now, or they'll chase us out into the open as my father and I do the hares.

"Move together," I say sharply. "Back-to-back."

We rush toward one another, backs pressed together. Pilot waves the torch from side to side, the flame dangerously low. After several horrible minutes, we begin to relax.

"What if they're still out there?" The terror on Elton's face dances in the fire's glow.

"They were just getting a look at us," Ms. Wade says, shuddering. "They haven't done anything to anyone. Let's remember that."

"They're growing more aggressive," Mr. Foster says.

"Nonsense." Ms. Wade presses her lips into a tight line, but even I can see her doubt. "Wolves don't hunt people. Not here at least. I've never heard of an Alaskan wolf biting a human. That thing with Elton, they were just chasing him 'cause he ran. And they smelled the venison on Mr. Foster. That's all."

Mr. Foster approaches Ms. Wade carefully. Then, slowly, he removes his jacket and pulls up the sleeve of his sweater. A sock is wrapped around his arm, right below the elbow. And beneath that—red and swollen—are teeth marks.

"I tried to clean it . . ." Mr. Foster's voice trails off.

My hands shake, and my throat tightens. The wolves bit through his jacket and sweater and every last piece of clothing he's wearing, and still managed to puncture his skin. How did I miss the torn fabric?

"They got at you," Nash says. For the first time, he doesn't laugh or add a witty remark. "That's why you been holding that arm."

Many emotions flicker across Ms. Wade's face as she studies Mr. Foster's wound—

Shock. Disbelief. Concern.

And then, finally, acceptance.

"We've got to get more tinder for the torch," Elton says.

Nash stares into the woods, searching for those yellow eyes. "How? They're probably still out there. Just smelling us and biding their time."

"If we don't get more," Elton insists, "the fire may go out before it's light."

"We stay put." Ms. Wade's voice is different. She knows the wolves aren't merely watching us. They're following us. *Stalking* us. They've bitten Mr. Foster and may have done worse if he hadn't fallen off that ledge.

One by one, we settle ourselves back onto the ground. I grip my father's gun until my knuckles whiten. Mr. Foster holds my .22 mag. I can't stop staring at him holding that rifle—clumsy, his hands in all the wrong places. It's disturbing to see such fear on my teacher's face, someone who always has the answer.

I don't close my eyes as we wait for the sun to rise.

Not once.

CHAPTER NINETEEN

I am exhausted as we locate the shelter we missed last night. My legs shake from exhaustion and lack of food. The cold wraps around my waist and squeezes like one of those man-eating snakes. I can't think past the chattering of my teeth. The aching in my muscles. I need sleep. And food. And warmth.

I need my dad, and my sister too.

The blizzard has passed us by, but it left behind a bone-deep chill, two feet of snow, and broken spirits. We'd celebrate if we weren't so exhausted.

I forget my own discomfort when Pilot removes his gloves. He's hunched over, trying to inspect his fingers in private. But I see them all the same. They're too red in places, and there's a spot on his thumb that looks bruised. No blisters yet. But he's going to have frostbite if we don't get to Vernon quickly.

First though, we have to eat.

As I grab my .22 mag, a much-needed energy rushes through my arms. The weight of the gun in my hands is like waking up in the morning, safe and warm beneath a pile of blankets. A sense of calm settles between my shoulder blades.

"Put your gloves back on," I tell Pilot, nodding toward his hands. "Elton will build us another fire tonight."

"Easy for you to say." Elton rubs his eyes.

"There are more shelters beyond this one," Nash says, nodding to the flimsy structure. "But if we walk hard, we can bypass them all and make it to the river sooner." Nash casts a glance at Ms. Wade. "If we're not being slowed down."

"Just get us back on the right track," I say to Nash. "Think you can handle that?"

Mr. Foster smiles. Nash glares. And I lean my .22 against my shoulder.

"I'm going hunting," I announce, handing the rifle to Mr. Foster.

"Can I go with you?" Pilot asks.

Well, obviously. I've got my lasso around your waist.

"Me too." Elton says. His voice is so small this morning, so strange sounding, that I can't tell him no.

"I'll look for kindling for the boy's fire," Nash says. "And I'll babysit these three." He jabs a thumb at Mr. Foster, Ms. Wade, and the dog.

Ms. Wade ignores Nash and looks at me with a tired smile, her face so very pale. "You're the best of us, Sloan."

I return her smile, a little embarrassed, and march into the trees and away from our clearing, listening for the sound of Pilot's footsteps. And Elton's too. No way am I going out here alone. Even with a gun. Even without the wolves.

It doesn't take long before I find what I'm looking for. The grouse perches in the spruce tree. The bird, spotted in black and white, could feed me and Pilot both. And while seeing one doesn't guarantee you'll see another, it's a good sign there may be more.

I take aim as Pilot and Elton step back. It's a far shot, but this gun has more trajectory than you'd think. I see the bird in my scope, my mouth watering over the sight of its swollen belly. People are counting on me. I will not miss.

I pull the trigger.

A heartbeat after the bullet fires from my gun, the grouse flutters and falls.

"Yes!" Pilot exclaims. "You got it, Sloan."

I smile despite myself, happy to have his approval.

He scratches the back of his neck and walks toward the bird. "I don't know much about hunting. Or even shooting, really." Pilot laughs uncomfortably. "Must think I'm pretty useless, huh?"

I watch him, realizing I'm not the only one who's searching for approval. His brave orange color flickers.

I'm about to tell him that I think he's kind, and strong, and that fighting for things that are right as he does means more than being able to handle a rifle. But before I can get a word out, movement catches my attention. I swing to the left and spot a second grouse among the treetops.

I nuzzle my cheek against the barrel a second time, cock the gun, and still my thoughts. I caress that trigger until the gun strikes back like a cat tired of human hands. This bird doesn't even flutter. It simply falls toward the earth.

Before I can gather the bird, Elton says out of nowhere, "My head is all weird today. I don't think . . . I don't think we should have left town."

I look at him, set my jaw.

"We had heat there," he continues, his words coming faster as his panic grows. "Maybe not a lot, but even once it cut off we had walls. We could have built fires, and eaten the rest of the food from the store. At the very least, we should have gone back for the things in the trailer. Food and more bullets and that compass you had."

"Elton—" Pilot starts.

"No! We should have stayed! I'm hungry and tired and we have no idea how far we are from the river. What were we thinking? Why didn't we stay put? Maybe someone made it back from Vernon. Maybe they called in a plow." Elton looks at me as if this is my fault. Maybe it is. "We shouldn't be out here. Maybe we should go back."

As eager as I am to get Ms. Wade to safety, his words entice me in a way I can't explain. It *would* be easier to return home. To wait for someone to make their way to us, instead of the other way around.

"We're almost to the river," Pilot says simply, striding toward our second prize. He's nearly there—just about has his hands around the bird—when I see the wolf.

Its ears are laid back, tail tucked close to a lean body.

"Pilot, stop."

He sees what I see, and freezes. My ears ring as Pilot steps slowly backward, his eyes fixed on the gray wolf. I shouldn't be surprised to see it here, though my stomach twists all the same. It's that same young wolf I've seen before, the one with the sharp nose and strong hunting instincts. The same one I've seen bullied by its pack mates.

The wolf may be young, but she's large enough, and quick enough, to take any of us down. Her posture doesn't seem aggressive though. She trots sideways a few steps, glancing at the three of us in turn, and then at the grouse. Slowly, as I remind myself to breathe, the wolf stalks toward the bird.

She already has our meal between her teeth when a second wolf appears.

A larger wolf.

The first wolf drops the grouse and scampers back. Then, as if catching herself, she thinks better of the fearful message she's sending and returns to her place beside the fallen bird.

Pilot, Elton, and I are out of sight, though certainly not beyond their range of smell, when the rest of the wolves appear. They were there all along, I realize. Frightened by the sound of my gun, but drawn by hunger. Blood spreads from the plump bird into the snow as the wolves circle the prey. The larger wolf rushes toward the gray female, and snaps at her face.

She drops the bird, and the second wolf quickly snatches it up and carries it to the black alpha male—the same one that stopped to sniff the female I shot.

The gray wolf whines, and I feel myself angry on her behalf. I've seen that gray wolf hunt. Her eyes are the keenest, her sense of smell the strongest. They'll follow her on a hunt, so why won't they give her the respect she deserves?

As if reading my mind, the gray wolf runs toward the wolf that stole her bird. But when she gets within a few inches of the lighter-colored wolf, the animal turns sharply and nips the gray wolf's ear.

She yelps and backs up, and I think for a moment that it's over. The pup's fear will get the best of her again, and her hunting will go unnoted. But when the lighter wolf drops the grouse at the alpha's feet, and is rewarded with a lick to her jaw, the gray wolf growls low in her throat. It sounds like the first real growl she's ever released, like there's nearly two years' worth of fear and frustration bottled inside her.

We edge farther away, but our steps are slow. We're terrified by the idea of so many wolves in one place, but there's also an energy that keeps our eyes locked on the animals.

The gray wolf raises her head, ears up, tail straight out from her body.

The lighter wolf matches her posture, her larger head held a touch higher.

Teeth bared.

Hackles raised.

The two wolves charge toward each other.

The gray wolf springs onto the back of the lighter wolf, but that wolf growls and twists away, biting the gray wolf on the neck as she spins. The gray wolf yelps, and the lighter wolf dashes out of reach.

The other wolves watch, beautifully still. They don't make a move to help their pack mates, recognizing that the battle is for rank. We stand frozen. Pilot's hand is in mine. I don't know how it got there, but I squeeze his fingers and move closer to Elton. My heart thumps so intensely that they must feel it.

I grip my gun until my arm shakes.

One bullet remains.

And look how many wolves. One, three, five, eight—

I stop counting when the lighter wolf launches an attack. Rearing onto her opponent's back, the lighter wolf raises her nose to the sky. The gray wolf reaches her head back and bites the lighter wolf's leg. Using her strong, youthful jaws, she yanks the other wolf off and throws her to the ground.

For one moment, I think it's over—the gray wolf will go for the lighter wolf's throat as I saw her do with the hare. But instead, the lighter wolf bounds onto her feet. My stomach drops like a stone, and the lighter wolf soars back on top. Her head is high, high, high. And though the gray wolf snarls and snaps at the older wolf, she remains in place. After a few seconds, the gray wolf's growling becomes less threatening, and more desperate.

My entire body tightens with anticipation and terror. As I watch the two wolves battle for dominance, all I can think is—

One bullet.

One bullet.

One bullet.

Not a strong bullet. Not for a wolf.

The gray wolf slinks backward at last, head lowered. But I see the way the other wolves look at her, with interest, with curiosity. The gray wolf lost her scuffle with her older pack mate, but she gained a new respect from her family. The alpha strides toward the young wolf, and though I expect her to tuck tail, she simply lowers her head.

I don't move a muscle, waiting to see what will happen. The alpha stands very still for several moments, and then sniffs a wound on the young wolf's check. He licks her there once, twice. The other wolves see their leader's response, and they start to sniff and lick and jump around their pack mates, releasing their nervousness, having enjoyed the entertainment, but also happy that peace has returned to the group.

I do not know the things Ms. Wade does about these wolves, but what happened just now—I understand it as if I grew up running alongside them. They are not so mysterious after all.

The alpha wolf takes the grouse in his jaws and the pack moves toward him. I notice the spaces between their ribs, and how eager they are for this meal. When one of the wolves, a male that stays close to the alpha, raises his nose and turns his head in our direction, I realize he knew we were there the entire time. They all did.

A shiver works its way down my spine as I tell Pilot, "Drop the grouse."

"No," he says firmly. "They take one, we take one."

I grab the grouse from him and throw it five feet. One of the wolves lowers its muzzle, curious. But now more of them move toward us. The smell of blood is in the air, and no matter how still we stand, we ooze fear. Wolves may not target humans when there's another option, but we can't be stupid.

"Move slowly," Pilot whispers to Elton and me. "Don't turn your back."

"I won't," I reply, raising my gun.

We stake a small step back. Then another. And another. The wolves snatch the second grouse and, after casting one last look in our direction, trot away into the woods.

"Why did that small wolf attack that other one?" Pilot whispers. "It could have been killed."

"Maybe it was just tired of being afraid," I reply so quietly I wonder if he hears.

Elton cranes his neck toward where we last saw the wolves. "Maybe they'll go away now."

But I don't respond. Because I'm worried that what actually happened was we reminded the wolves how good it feels to eat. Worse yet, I'm afraid we created an association for the wolves—

Smelling humans.

Feeding their stomachs.

These things belong together.

Pilot, Elton, and I walk in silence until we hear the sound of Mr. Foster yelling.

We exchange a worried glance, and then we're running, our legs carrying us through the snow as fast as we can go.

CHAPTER TWENTY

We're almost back to the shelter when I hear a new sound. My entire body goes numb, and I wish I were deaf in both ears. Wish I couldn't hear the terrible noise I've learned to recognize—

The static of wolves.

Mere seconds after I hear them, I spot them. The same wolves that stole our birds. They crowd inside the shelter, growling and tugging at a large shape on the floor. Five wolves work their powerful jaws into Ms. Wade and tug backward, digging their paws into the snow, trying desperately to pull her from the shelter.

Elton screams and the dog barks and Nash appears from out of nowhere, a confused look on his face. Mr. Foster aims my daddy's gun like he's trying to use it, but the safety is still on.

My legs turn to pudding, and a cry rips from my throat. One of the wolves raises its head at the noise, muzzle covered in red. That's the sight that sets me in motion—Ms. Wade's blood on that wolf's lips.

I toss my .22 to the ground and snatch the rifle from Mr. Foster. My legs tremble and tears sting my eyes and my throat burns. But my hands are steady on that gun. My gaze finds those crosshairs and the world stops tilting.

I pull the trigger.

And the largest wolf falls.

The remaining wolves leap to the side and start to retreat. But hunger keeps them lurking at the edges of the trees. They sniff the air, whining. That's *their* meal, and we're attempting to take it.

"No!" I roar, grabbing my .22. "You can't have her!"

I line up a second shot on the alpha. Our eyes meet, my brown to his yellow.

I see you now.

I pull the trigger.

The alpha male darts to the side, but he doesn't move fast enough. I graze his back leg, and he releases a yelp of surprise. This time, the wolves don't hesitate. They race into the forest and camouflage themselves among the trees. The alpha goes with them, limping and bleeding into the snow.

"We were only gone a second," Mr. Foster says, shaking.

But it doesn't matter.

Ms. Wade's leg sticks out from the doorway, her pant leg

raised to the knee. Pale skin glows in the morning air. Even from here, I can see the teeth marks above her sock hem.

Elton is first to the shelter, until Mr. Foster grabs him by the shoulders and guides him out. The boy takes three quick steps in my direction and throws himself at me. When his knees buckle, and he's too heavy for me to hold up, I guide us both to the ground. Though I turn my face away, I can't cry.

Deep inside my chest, a layer of ice rises from Sloan the Brave's ashes. It crawls over my heart the same way it did when my mother left. When Pilot drops down beside us and puts his arms around me, the tears still don't come.

He holds Elton and me for another moment before I pull away and walk toward the shelter.

"Just stay back," Nash says. But what does he care?

Nash reaches out to touch me but—*oh, look!*—I remember the gun. One bullet. That's all we have remaining, and I've got it aimed at Nash like it was his teeth that tore into the only semblance of a mother I had left in this world.

Nash raises his hands as I train my daddy's gun.

No, not my daddy's gun.

This *was* my grandfather's gun.

This *was* my father's gun.

Now it's *my* gun.

The old Sloan carried a .22 fit for rabbits and squirrels and quail. This Sloan uses the gun she needs and doesn't hesitate to take down a grown wolf, or a grown *man*, if they pose a risk to those she loves.

I stare at Nash before lowering the rifle and striding forward. When my eyes fall on Ms. Wade, my stomach threatens to upend itself. Good thing there's nothing in there.

Ms. Wade is missing the glove on her right hand, and it's clear a wolf was yanking on her wrist. Her jacket is torn open, and the layers beneath are lifted so that I can see white, creamy infection oozing from those four holes in her side. There are no teeth marks on her stomach, and for some reason that comforts me.

Her legs are another matter.

From hips to ankles, her pants, jeans, and thermals are torn through. In one place above her knee, I can see where a wolf became too impatient to wait for its meal. Ms. Wade stares blankly at the ceiling, and though I may be imagining it, she seems peaceful.

Please let her have died before the wolves came.

It's heartbreaking, that this can be my only hope for her. Not that she was surrounded by her boys when she went, and maybe by a few of those little grandchildren. Not that she was in her own home, under a handmade quilt. But rather, that she wasn't alive when eaten by wolves.

"We have to bury her," I say, staring at that tender pink

color rolling off her that, in death, somehow shines even brighter.

Nash strips off Ms. Wade's jacket and tosses it to Pilot. Every nerve in my body strains to stop him as he pulled at her. But I remember Pilot's hands, and I know Ms. Wade would tell him to take it, that it's too cold out to act thickheaded.

Even with the five of us, we are only able to dig a couple of inches into the snow. We use rocks and sticks and our stiff fingers, but it's not nearly enough. Before we cover her, I lay my .22 mag across her chest and drape her arm over the barrel should she need it in the great beyond. Then we mark the surrounding trees so that we can find her when we return with help.

Mr. Foster stands at her head and speaks of a shepherd and green pastures. Of souls and the valley of the shadow of death. More words he undoubtedly read in a book. But I can't listen. If I do, the ice in my chest might melt. And I'll lie down next to Ms. Wade and won't move.

When Mr. Foster stops talking, Nash reminds us we are only a few stops from the river, that we'll be in Vernon tomorrow night now that we can travel faster.

My hands clench at his attitude.

The basset hound puts its nose to the fallen wolf we've

ignored, and sniffs. Then he yaps twice before Pilot picks him up and holds him close.

With hunger gnawing at my gut, and sorrow threatening to overtake my body, I take the first step away from Ms. Wade.

Mr. Foster bows his head. "Goodbye, Norma Jean."

We've walked maybe thirty feet before we hear the excited howls. Before we turn and see—far in the distance—those greedy wolves digging up Ms. Wade.

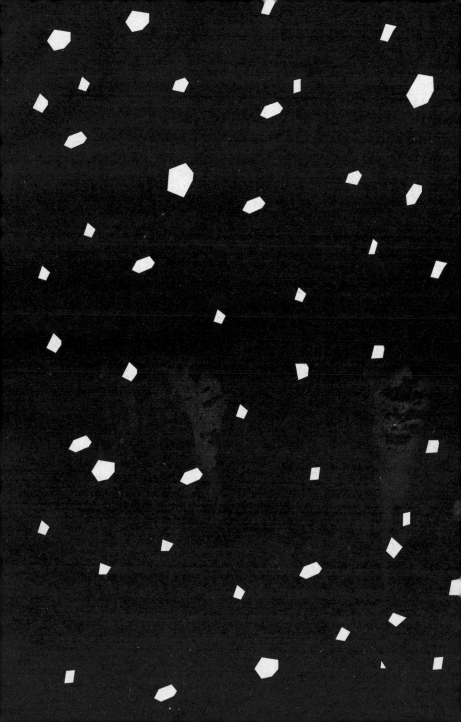

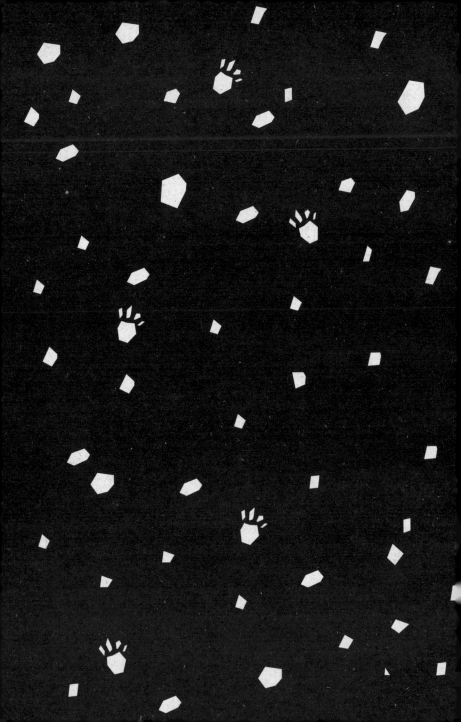

CHAPTER

TWENTY-ONE

Keep going. Get to the river. One foot in front of the other. I hold these commands in my mind, repeating them over and over, and I'm able to move my right foot, then my left. Right, left. Right, left.

Elton's stomach growls, causing my own to clench and cramp. As the snow drifts lazily over our shoulders, I keep my head down and focus on what it will be like to have my father and sister by my side once again. The loss of Ms. Wade makes me want them here, now. But more than that, it makes me think of my mother. Of that day by the river. The sun shone through the trees like it was drawn to Mama as she lay on her back, hands tucked behind her head.

"What do you see when you look up?" she asked me.

I squinted at the leaves, wanting to please her with the right answer. "There's a beetle crawling on that tree. See it?" I pointed.

Mama's smile widened. "You notice the details in your surroundings; that's good. But what do you *feel*?"

I looked at the leaves again—orange and red and yellow—and I looked at the trees, old and wise and strong. I looked at the sky, the wisps of white clouds and a blueness so rich it looked like one of my mother's paintings. These things didn't make me feel much, but I knew that was wrong. So I peeked at Mama from the corner of my eye, her blond hair spread across the blanket. Her eyes bursting with life, when so many other days they were dull. Her slender hands beat a quiet rhythm on the ground beside her, and she radiated joy.

"I feel happy, Mama," I said quietly.

She turned her head toward me then, and her smile stretched all the way to my heart. Sitting up, she examined her ruby ring in the light. Then, with a beat of hesitation, she slipped it off her finger. "You should wear this today," she said, sliding it onto my thumb.

I curled my hand around it carefully, terrified it would fall off. How many times had I seen that ring bring a smile to Mama's face when it seemed nothing possibly could?

"Go and explore. I want to think on my next painting." She winked then. "Even brilliant artists such as ourselves need a plan when creating."

I wore that ring the rest of the morning, and through the afternoon. But I must have forgotten to keep my hand curled, because at one point I looked down and it was gone. I'll never forget the look on my mama's face when I told her I'd lost it. She tried to smile, to say she hated that old ring, but I saw the sadness creeping into her eyes once again. A sadness that didn't disappear for weeks after we returned from the river. A sadness that led Mama to leave us all behind.

I didn't force my mother to leave, I knew.

But I made her so sad she couldn't stay, and wasn't that the same thing?

Ms. Wade would tell me, *No, it's not the same thing at all.* And that is why I already miss her so much it makes my legs tremble.

"Look at that." Nash's voice tears me from my self-pity. He's pointing at something in the distance. When I peer closer, I make out what it is.

A wolf lies in a trap similar to the one we saw two days ago. And even though I just watched a half dozen of its kind getting at Ms. Wade, I still shudder at the sharp, glittering teeth snapped tight on the wolf's body.

As we plod closer, curiosity driving us to crane our necks, I realize the trap has the wolf's front legs in its grasp. Then I realize something else—

The wolf is breathing.

"It's alive," Elton says, bending down to inspect the animal.

"Not too close," I warn.

Elton remembers himself and pops upright. He steps backward, and I lay a hand on his shoulder. Elton stares at it with a strange look on his face. Like he's rarely been touched with kindness.

Pilot's voice grazes my good ear. "Sloan—"

The wolf stirs. It opens its eyes, sees us, and scratches at the snow with its back paws. The whine the animal releases cuts deep. I want to hate this creature. I want to kill it with the butt of my gun because it doesn't deserve a swift death.

But at the same time . . .

Those pleading eyes stare up at me with such terror. It's in impossible pain, half-starved, and now here we are—five humans looming over its trapped body. How threatening must we look? Can it see the hunger in our eyes?

My tongue flicks unconsciously over my split, bleeding lips, and my stomach rumbles imagining the wolf crackling over one of Elton's fires. I'd spare a shirt to get the fire started. I might burn every last scrap of clothing I have if it meant a full belly.

The wolf tries desperately to flee, but after it strains against the trap, those awful teeth ripping through its legs, the wolf yelps and collapses. Lying on its side, the wolf stares up at me with one darting yellow eye. Its chest heaves as I bend down, studying it closely.

You killed her, I think, though I know it isn't true.

"Maybe . . . maybe we should leave it," Mr. Foster says quietly.

I hold my rifle across my chest like a pageant queen's sash, and find that no matter how much anger I hold, I can still see past my sorrow to the frightened animal. This wolf is alone. Abandoned by its brothers and sisters, its family pack. How many days has it spent out here alone in the cold? Had it given up before we arrived?

If we would kill this animal in order to survive, my mind whispers, *then are we so different?*

I rise to my feet, and the wolf fights against the trap a third time.

I turn around to say . . . what? That we should leave it? That we should free it?

That we should treat it the same way its pack mates treated Ms. Wade?

But when I look behind me, all I see is Nash Blake. He's powering toward the animal, arms raised above his head.

"What are you—?"

The look on Nash's face is wild, not quite human. His lips pull back from his teeth and his eyes are as round as the stone between his hands. He brings his arms down, quick. I hear the sickening thud as he smashes the rock against the wolf's rib cage.

Shock shoots through me, sets my heart to racing, and Pilot's dog to barking. I grab Nash's arm and try to pull him from the wolf, but he turns and shoves me with all his strength. I fly backward, hit my head against a tree. The wolf's panicked cries ring through my skull as Nash brings the rock down again and again, until everything is quiet.

Nash's chest rises and falls rapidly while he wipes the wolf's blood from his face and jacket. "There," he says as bile rises in my stomach. "Because none of you chickens would have done it."

"What is wrong with you?" I climb to my feet, one hand on my head.

Pilot reaches out to steady me, eerily quiet.

Nash scoffs. "Let me guess? You would have rather used our last remaining bullet to do the job."

I point at Nash. "You didn't just kill him. You beat that wolf to death for fun."

"Look, I'm hungry!" Nash roars. "And I'm tired of being out here. We need to eat. We need to move. And we need to get to Vernon. I don't . . . I don't feel good, all right? It's a shame what happened to that woman, but she was old. Her husband was already in the ground, and now she is too. They're together. That's a good thing, right?"

Nash tosses the rock onto the ground and dusts his hands off.

And Pilot points my gun at his father.

CHAPTER

TWENTY-TWO

"There *is* something wrong with you," Pilot says, his voice flat. "You're not like the rest of us. You must see that."

"Pilot . . ." I try to get my gun back, but he steps toward his father.

"This is the second time today you've had this gun pointed at you," he continues.

Nash raises his hands, slowly.

"Sooner or later," Pilot adds, "someone's going to pull the trigger. I'm not saying it's going to be me, because I got Mom to think about. But I want you to remember I pointed it at you. I want you to remember I had my finger on the trigger."

The basset hound whines at Pilot's feet, and the boy lowers the rifle. I snatch it from him.

Nash rolls his shoulders back and stares down his nose at his son. "You think I'm scared of you? You think having a gun makes you a tough guy?" Nash smiles his nasty smile.

"You hate me, that's fine. I know I wasn't a good dad. Better than my own, mind you. But I'm sick and tired of you hanging on your mama like she never did a wrong thing in her life."

Nash scratches his forehead, leaving behind a streak of sticky red blood. He opens his mouth to say something, and stops himself. Then opens it a second time. My stomach flips wondering what's so horrible that even Nash hesitates to say it aloud.

"You know your mama didn't want you, right?" Nash says, his words a bullet through our hearts. "She told me so. Said it every day until you showed up."

Pilot shakes his head. "Shut up."

"Sure, after you was born she decided to be mother of the year and all that. But that was only 'cause she felt sorry for you. We could see you weren't smart right from the beginning."

"Stop lying!" Pilot yells.

"That kind of regret? Not wanting a baby even when it's yours? You can't tell me that feeling goes away. Not completely."

"That's enough," Mr. Foster says, but he doesn't move. We're all frozen. Linked by a feeling that this moment between father and son is dangerous, and that if we say the wrong thing? Step in the wrong place?

Boom.

"You've been a burden on your mama since the beginning. And maybe you hated me, but at least I wanted you. At least I didn't curse your existence."

Pilot's arms tighten at his sides. His teeth grind.

Pilot is a bomb tick-tick-ticking.

And his daddy? Well, he's the man pulling the clip with his teeth.

Pilot's basset hound presses against the side of my leg, aware of the tension and afraid. Always afraid.

Elton squares his slim shoulders, dusted by the snow. "You know what I think?" the boy says to Nash. "I think you're sad. You're sad because if you die like Ms. Wade, no one will care." Elton lets that sink in, and Nash's face scrunches like Elton is an idiot. But I see it. I see in the man's eyes that he's thinking on this. "Pilot would be upset though. If you died. No one would understand why, but he would be."

Nash looks from Elton to Pilot, and as much as he tries to hide the reaction, I can see that what Nash wants more than anything—more than getting to Vernon or winning Pilot's mama back or having a bowl of roasted lamb right this very second—is for Pilot to say it's true.

But Pilot only squares his shoulders, looks his father dead in the face for a long moment, and then turns and walks away.

This time, I know exactly what to do. I follow him. Not because my lasso is around his waist. But because one winter day two years ago he reminded me that people care.

And now it's time to repay the favor.

I find Pilot sitting in the snow, back against a tree, head in his hands. His dog sits between his legs, wet nose resting on his knee.

"There you are, dog. I've been looking all over for you." I act surprised to see Pilot. "Oh, hello to you too, I suppose."

My joke falls flat.

I squat down beside Pilot, moving close enough that our arms touch before I can overthink it. "You want me to go away?"

Pilot shrugs, but he also lifts his head. "The worst part is I know he's telling the truth. My dad is a bad person, but he's not a liar."

I chew my lip, feeling like this is bigger than I am. If Ms. Wade were here . . .

I shake my head and push down the sadness and shock of what happened to her, and try to focus on Pilot. "So . . ." I start carefully, "what if your mom *didn't* want you in the beginning?"

Pilot winces, and I think, *Stupid, stupid.*

"What I mean to say is, sometimes people don't know

they want something until they get it. And maybe that thing for your mom was you."

Farts moves in front of me and lies down on my boots, getting his dog slobber all over them. I rub a hand over his back because I know the animal is every bit as cold and hungry as we are.

When Pilot doesn't respond, I keep flapping my lips. "It's like with you," I say with a small smile. "When you . . . when you found me. I hated you, right? I hated that you saw me when I was weak. I hated seeing you every day after that because it reminded me of something ugly."

"Is this supposed to make me feel better?"

"The thing is," I continue, concern making my tongue thick, "I guess I started to like you somewhere along the way. I mean, I still told myself I hated you. But I knew I didn't." I take a deep breath. "Seeing you at school every day? It reminded me that someone out there cared."

"I looked for you all day when you were lost," Pilot says, his voice small. "At night too. I was furious that we weren't doing a real search. All of us in a line and stuff."

I lay my hand on Pilot's arm. My fingers tingle where they touch his jacket. "I think your mama was scared about bringing you into a life that had your daddy in it. But once you were here . . . Oh, Pilot. Can't you see how much she loves you? You saved her. If it weren't for you, she'd never have left that trailer, would never have started selling goods out of that little barn."

"My aunt sent money so Mom could build it into a proper store," Pilot says, almost smiling. "That made my dad so mad."

I nod and give Farts a good scratch behind his ears.

When I glance over at Pilot, I find him staring at me.

"Did you really want me to leave you out there?" he all but whispers. "That morning I found you, you said—"

"I remember what I said." I turn away, shame coloring my face.

"Did you mean it?" he asks softly.

I chew the inside of my cheek. Think about keeping that humiliation inside, where I can feed it and care for it and watch it grow. But instead, I say, simply, quietly, "Yeah. I did."

Pilot nods like this makes sense. Then he fills his lungs, scrunches up his face, and replies, "I was thinking stuff like that when you gave me those gloves."

I look at him square in the eyes, and he gives another small nod as if to tell me it's true.

My skin burns knowing this new information about Pilot. I'm sad for him, but also relieved that I'm not alone. That I wasn't the only kid in Rusic thinking thoughts dark enough to swallow me whole and stop my heart. Heck, maybe there are hundreds of kids in the world like Pilot and me. Maybe thousands. All of us just dangling from silver threads, fearing—and sometimes hoping—that someone will cut the strings and we'll all fall down.

Before I can think better of it, before I remember the scared girl I've become, my color so yellow it glitters, I lean over and kiss Pilot on the cheek. His skin is impossibly cold beneath my lips, but I don't cut the gesture short. I stay there for a moment—pulse racing, skin tingling—and let him know I mean it.

When I pull back, Pilot's eyes are big with surprise. He searches my face for a long time. So long I forget how to breathe. Then he looks down at his hands as I silently urge the abominable snowman to snatch me up, chomp on my head, and save me from my mortification.

"I'm sorry," I say. "I shouldn't have—"

Pilot turns toward me suddenly and takes my face in his hands and kisses me on the lips. Like, his lips on my lips and both of us closing our eyes but I kind of crack my eyes to make sure this is really happening.

It's over quick. Too soon, maybe. Definitely too soon.

Pilot smiles at me like a sheep dog that nipped the one thing it's supposed to watch over. "No," he says. "*I'm* sorry."

I grin into my hands, and Farts cocks his head at us and I wish so bad my stupid sister were here so I could tell her what happened. Even if she'd pretend I was a child and act like she didn't care. Even then.

Mr. Foster appears, and my face turns the color of August raspberries. He grins like he knows something even though I may die of embarrassment if he does. Just as soon though, a furrowed brow replaces his smile.

"We should get going." My teacher clears his throat. Looks directly at me. "Elton is talking about the wolf. Wondering what to do with it."

I know what he's asking, and why he's asking me. I'm the daughter of a butcher, after all. My insides churn, but when I see the dark circles beneath Mr. Foster's eyes, and hunger twists inside my own belly, I know what has to be done.

So I stand up, take a deep breath, and walk back toward the others. And after I show them the best way, everyone pitches in to help prepare the meat. I check it twice to be sure it looks safe, and Elton uses Ms. Wade's jacket to start a fire.

Then we eat. In absolute silence, we eat. And after we're done, we brush ourselves off and turn away.

Even Nash remains quiet as we trek toward the river.

CHAPTER

TWENTY-THREE

As the sun arcs toward the earth, I stand with my toes at the edge of a frozen river.

Mr. Foster looks at us hopefully, but no one is celebrating. This isn't the river we were aiming for, just one of the bigger streams that feeds into it. We shouldn't have reached this far north. I suspected we were off course when I saw the ravine, but now I'm certain.

"Great job," Pilot tells his father. "But not the river we wanted."

"Is there a bridge somewhere we could cross?" Mr. Foster asks.

"Don't be stupid." Nash cocks his head at the man. "Want to spend another night in the snow?"

My mind zips to the wolves, and already I'm searching the surface, trying to convince myself the ice is thick enough to cross.

Elton sighs. He's disappointed we walked so far out of our way.

Pilot rubs his thumb into the palm of his right hand and winces. Nash has a point. We can't sleep in the elements a second time. And so I touch the butt of my rifle to the edge of the pond. I press down with my body, and when I don't hear any shifting, I take a tentative step.

"Sloan, I should go first," Pilot says.

I shoot him a look that says I won't be underestimated. I have a fear of being alone, fine. But that doesn't mean I can't be brave. Besides, I know how to get across. *The ice can be thinner in some places than others*, Daddy told me once. *So watch for movement. Listen for cracking.*

Elton is the next to step out onto the ice, with a careful Mr. Foster close on his heels. Pilot and his dog go next.

I walk back and forth along the edge of the river, moving a few feet farther out each time. Bending the right side of my face toward the ice, I listen. But I know one good ear isn't enough. Not now.

I glance at Pilot. "Can you—?"

"I'm listening." Pilot nods to his dog. "He may not be good for much, but if that ice cracks, he'll hear it."

And so I continue, slowly—like *heart in my throat I can barely breathe* slowly—toward the opposite side of the river.

I watch the basset hound as he sniffs the ice, ears drooping. We've made it fifteen feet across, moving back and forth, when a low whine escapes the dog's throat.

My head whips around as chills shoot across my skin. Everyone stops, arms flying out to our sides as if that'll somehow keep us from falling in. The dog stares back at us, whining nervously, and I realize it isn't the ice he's warning us about.

"It's his paws." Pilot puts both arms beneath the dog and hoists him up with a grunt. "The ice is colder than the snow."

"Oh." I turn back to the ice, worried that we just lost our best alarm, and knowing I have to continue anyway.

Mr. Foster skims forward. "Seriously, Sloan. Let me go first. I've studied weather patterns, including how to—"

"You spend six good years studying these woods?" Pilot asks.

I look Mr. Foster square in the eyes. Pull myself upright. "I've got this."

He examines my face. Then he nods.

"Enough chatter," Nash says, a shade less confident. "Get us across this thing."

My neck tingles as I take another step. And another. Each time, I touch my rifle in the place I plan to step as if that will somehow protect me.

I've got a gun, you hear? No funny business!

We've got to be halfway across when a cracking sound reaches my ear.

"Sloan, stop," Elton says in a fierce whisper, because we've heard tales of breaking through ice with a simple raised voice.

A bolt of panic shoots through me, toes to nose, and I stop cold. The noise comes again, and I try to pinpoint where it stems from, my pulse pounding along my neck. Several seconds pass. Or maybe it's hours. Maybe it's centuries and we're all made of stone now so what does it matter?

Slowly, the fear creeping across my scalp slithers away. I hold my rifle out, slow enough to catch a black fly, and tap on that ice.

Tap, tap, tap.

No one moves.

Tap, tap, tap.

I watch the worried faces of my companions. When Pilot nods, I step out onto the next patch of ice. My foot lands solid, and so I shift my weight. When we've gone another five or six feet, Elton laughs nervously. Mr. Foster joins him.

Nash tells them to stop being morons, but even I can hear the relief in his voice.

I keep my eyes on the frozen surface. Glide one foot after the other. Not too much weight until I'm sure.

Tap, tap, tap.

Test, test.

There.

When I glance up, I realize we're almost out of harm's way. The shore is six feet away. Maybe less. Sensation tingles into my arms and legs. I hadn't felt the numbness rolling over me until now.

We're so close that Pilot sets his dog back down. The basset hound races across the ice, slipping and sliding a little before finally reaching the edge. As soon as he's safe on solid ground, the dog lifts his nose and howls.

Did you see what I did there? he seems to say. *Raced ahead of you all. I'm a good dog. Good dog!*

Laughter thunders from Pilot, mostly because that howl is followed by Farts tucking his tail and cowering, as if his own vocal chords make him nervous.

I throw Pilot a grin, and Pilot shrugs like, *What can you do about such an idiot animal? I love him.*

My eyes are still on Pilot when I hear the cracking.

Did I forget to tap? Did I forget to test?

Doesn't matter now.

The ice starts to split beneath our feet. No one moves. No one breathes. For a moment, nothing happens. Then the ice cracks cheerfully, as if it waited until we thought we were safe.

I glance down, my body shaking with fear. The ice is solid beneath my boots. Pilot seems stable too. So do Nash and Mr. Foster.

But Elton stares at his feet. At the small veins forming between his boots.

The ice cracks, snaps, pops—

And then tears open beneath Elton.

"No!" I scream. A rift rips the frozen surface into pieces, and I throw myself onto my stomach. "Get down! Get down!"

Elton's right leg plummets into the slushy water, but he dives at the last possible moment and is able to pull free. He stretches out like I have, arms and legs spread wide as if we're skydiving.

Pilot is on his stomach.

Mr. Foster is too.

Nash stands frozen, arms straight out on either side. He looks to me in that moment like the man on the cross in our chapel.

The ice breaks beneath Nash's feet.

And he's gone.

CHAPTER
TWENTY-FOUR

The water releases a satisfied slurp as it swallows Nash Blake. Elton scrambles on his belly toward the opening, horror twisting his face.

"Elton, no," I bark. "Don't move. Don't anyone move."

Pilot ignores me and squirms on his stomach, grunting, his breath coming in panicked bursts.

"Dad?" he yells. "Dad!"

Pilot plunges his arm into the water up to the shoulder.

"Stop!" I yell, thinking of his hands.

Pilot brings his arm out, unsuccessful, before plunging it back in. He screams with frustration, and the ice crackles beneath his body. Beneath all of us.

"Pilot, get away from there," Mr. Foster bellows.

But Pilot is still searching, still screaming, his sentences broken.

"Useless idiot!" Pilot grumbles. ". . . don't you dare. Drunken. Skinny jerk . . ."

Seconds turn to minutes. How long has his dad been under? One minute? Three?

Too long.

I cinch my eyes shut. I hate Nash, but I don't want him dead. Not after Ms. Wade. Not this way. Not with Pilot trying to rescue him.

"YOU WILL NOT DIE, YOU MONSTER!" Pilot roars.

Nash Blake flies upward, sputtering water, his jacket twisted in his son's fist.

"Haaa!" I scream.

For one blissful moment, Pilot's face beams with joy. He's so happy to see his father alive. So stupidly, brilliantly happy.

And then Nash grabs on to his son and drags him forward. Pilot tries to scramble backward, but Nash yanks harder, using his son's weight to free himself from the water. But in doing so, he's pulling Pilot in.

Their bodies are a blur against the ice, arms flailing, fingers scratching. I don't know how it happens. I don't know how I end up on my knees, hands cradling my rifle, the crosshairs on Pilot's father.

Will I do it?

Can I do it?

If I don't take him out, he'll kill his own son. Nash gets a better hold, his hands clutching Pilot's shoulders. His jaw is set, and as Pilot's arms splash downward, and Nash rises like a ghost from the grave, I release a bloodcurdling scream.

My finger tickles that trigger.

I don't have a choice, do I? My lasso is around Pilot. I cannot live without my lasso. I cannot live without Pilot Blake, who carried me from the woods.

Pilot cries out, and in a desperate attempt to survive, he reaches back and hits his father clean between the eyes. Nash's head snaps backward and he loses his grip.

Pilot scrambles away from his father, panting. I expect Nash to disappear beneath the ice again, but he doesn't. He clings to the edge, and slowly, he grows still.

"Help me, Pilot," he says, though I can barely understand him through the chattering of his teeth. His skin is blue, his eyes half-closed.

He reaches one hand out to his son, but Pilot only scrunches up his nose.

"Pilot," I say, struck with an idea. He glances at me, and I slide the rifle toward him real slow, so very careful not to disrupt the ice.

Pilot snatches it and starts to stretch it toward his father. But then he stops. Stops and stares at Nash as if seeing him for the first time. His eyes widen and his chest heaves and I realize he's about to do something awful.

"Pilot, reach it toward him," I say.

But Pilot doesn't move. He just watches as his father closes his eyes and lays his head down on the ice. Nash's fingers slip from the edge one at a time.

Thumb. Pinkie. Pointer.

"Pilot, help him!" Elton yells.

"Give him the rifle," I echo, because Pilot won't be himself if he lets this happen. He won't be the boy who gave his mama the courage to start again. He won't be the boy who left a note in my bag at school that said, *Thanks for the gloves. Can I go hare hunting with you sometime?*

And so I yell at him to help his father. I yell and yell and when still he stares at his father as the last of Nash's fingers slips from the ice, I dive toward the man. I grab Nash by the collar and yank him upward. I can only manage to raise him a few inches, but seeing me pull his father from the ice chases away the ugly in Pilot, and he grabs his dad too.

Between the two of us, with Mr. Foster chanting *careful, careful*, we manage to free Nash from the ice. And because Nash is stubborn as a mule, he kicks to his feet, and half walks, half staggers as Pilot and I lead him toward the snowy shore.

CHAPTER

TWENTY-FIVE

My mind is fuzzy and my body is exhausted. But with Nash mumbling which way to go, we're able to find our way again, reaching the next shelter with sunlight to spare. Pilot has his arm beneath his father's shoulders, and Mr. Foster has the man's opposite side. All of us besides Elton have threatened Nash. And yet we can't leave him behind. I can hear the wolves howling, like they know one of us has weakened, and they lick their chops eagerly, waiting for him to fall.

Nash slumps to the floor, and his head sags to his chest.

"We've got to get him warm," Elton says.

"Do we?" Pilot mutters.

I stare at Pilot, shocked at his coldness, but understanding it all the same.

"We need to build a fire." Elton looks at each of us in turn. At the clothing on our backs. Then he looks down at his own jacket. When he starts to reach for his zipper, Mr. Foster stops him.

"No, not you. You make the fire. That's enough." He lowers his eyes, but I don't miss the shame in them. "It's time I do something to help."

He rips off his jacket, and then pulls a sweater over his head. Beneath that is a long-sleeved thermal, teeth marks torn into the fabric. A dark stain spreads from his elbow, and I wonder just how bad that bite has become.

Elton takes Pilot and they return with two rocks. They clear a spot directly outside the door, covering it with dry wood from inside the shelter and crisp dead leaves that snuck in.

"Couldn't find two flints. But this one has quartz in it. See?" Elton holds up a stone that looks as if it contains crystals. Then he starts swiping the smoother, grayer stone against the other. Once again, it takes forever. The entire time, Nash moans and shakes and leans against the shelter wall. When at last a spark lights, we dry Mr. Foster's thermal and feed it to the flames. Nash leans forward, blocking anyone else from reaching the heat.

"Should he . . . should he take his clothes off?" I whisper, as if Nash can't hear.

Elton looks at the man, and says firmly, "Yeah, he should."

But Nash doesn't move, and neither do we.

Mr. Foster leans back and sighs, the weight of the day taking its toll.

"That was cool of you," Elton says to Mr. Foster. "To offer your shirt so I didn't have to give mine."

"It's the least I could do." Mr. Foster opens his mouth to add more, but hesitates. Making up his mind, he says, "I've always been more intelligent than those around me. By the time I was thirteen, my own parents couldn't keep up with my learning. But out here"—he waves his hands toward the door—"I'm completely lost." His eyes flick in my direction. "I feel stupid."

I cringe. "Why'd you do that? Why'd you look at me when you said *stupid*? I'm not dumb, you know. I can do things."

"Yes, you can. I see that now. You're in your element in these woods."

"Maybe you were wrong about me," I whisper, staring down at my hands.

"I was definitely wrong about you," he admits. "You know, there are these standardized tests that can measure what a person will excel at academically. But they can't test for ambition." He sighs. "And there's definitely no test that measures how well a person can survive these kinds of circumstances. I'm not sure where we'd be without you, Sloan."

I glance at Pilot, and though I know he's fit to burst with anger, he nods to say it's true. My cheeks blaze.

"I said you were brave," Elton adds. "I said it first."

"I don't feel brave," I say quietly. "Or *vulnerable*, or whatever."

Mr. Foster frowns. "Well, those words don't mean the same thing."

I shoot him a look, and he holds his hands up as if to apologize. I lick my lips and say, "No, what do you mean?"

My teacher lowers his hands. "Well, uh, being brave means you show a sense of courage in a dangerous situation, or a situation you perceive to be dangerous. But vulnerability? That's putting yourself in a position to be harmed, but usually for the purposes of benefiting. It's like falling in love. You might get hurt, but then you might find happiness." Mr. Foster looks at Pilot and his eyes seem to smile.

I fidget, and though I'm not angry, my words sound that way when I say, "And *intuitive*? I guess you think that doesn't mean *smart*."

"Not exactly, no. Intuition is knowing something without evidence. Like when you knew where to step on the ice even though there were no markers." Mr. Foster squints. "You're probably one of the most intuitive kids I've met."

My heart swells until I don't think there's room for it to stay put. Because if his definition is right, then I *have* been vulnerable. Loving my mother and losing her did that. And

Mr. Foster thinks I'm intuitive. Maybe not smart like him, but the kind of smart my mama said I'd need.

"You really want to be an artist?" Mr. Foster asks softly.

I stare at him hard. Don't answer.

"Because if you do," he says, "then I think you'll be successful. Like I said, no one can measure ambition."

"Sometimes ambition is ugly though, right?" Pilot challenges, startling me. "Like when ambitious wolves manage to drag an old woman from where she lays dying? Or when a man beats a wolf to death to quench his anger?" Pilot pauses, breathing hard. He turns a hard gaze on his father. "When a man tries to drag his only son into a frozen river to save himself? Is that ambition good?"

Mr. Foster considers Pilot. "That's not really ambition. It's more—"

But Nash cuts him off, saying, without turning around, "I wasn't thinking."

"Sure you were, Dad," Pilot snaps. "For once, you really were."

Nash shakes his head. "You should have let me die."

"Finally!" Pilot booms. "The man talks sense."

Nash shakes all over as he hunches toward the fire. He wipes his face real quick, but I can't see why he does it. "When your mother told me she was carrying, it made me so happy it was like I couldn't catch my breath. I wanted to do right by you. Get straight work. Make your mama happy so she'd see it was a good thing, you coming and all."

Pilot leans back, as if his father's sudden turn hurts him more than biting words.

"When you were born you were so small. I would hold you in my hands and stare at you and I'd get sick with how much *want* was in me." Nash keeps his face turned toward the fire as he speaks. "No matter how hard I tried though, I always messed up. I would forget to give you your milk when your mama went out, and one time I let you roll right off the bed. I may be dense, but even I could see you loved your mama more. I hated her for it because she was the one who didn't know about you in the beginning. So I started up again . . . What I mean is I started going to the tavern again to get my head right. But then that made you want your mama even more." Nash swallows. "I wanted you more than anything in the whole world. And you didn't want me back."

Nash turns from the fire and looks at his son. He holds Pilot's gaze and says, "I'm a waste of a father. But I didn't mean it back there. If I'd have killed you, I would've done myself in next."

Pilot's face pulls together, pained, and my own heart

clenches wondering how he must feel about his father saying something he's probably waited his whole life to hear. Pilot rolls his shoulders back, and instead of looking at Nash, he looks at me.

"We've got to get him to Vernon. He'll die out here if we don't keep moving."

Nash raises his fingers as if he might touch Pilot, but is worried what'll happen if he does.

Pilot snaps his own hand away. "Don't. We're not good. We'll never be good. I barely believe a word that comes out of your mouth." He pauses. "I'll get you to Vernon. After that, I want you to stay there. Don't come back to Rusic. If you do that for me . . . if you stay there and don't try to contact Mom or me or even *ask* about us, then maybe, and I do mean *maybe*, one day I'll look for you." Pilot sighs. "You sure you know the way to the last shelter? Can you find it in the dark?"

Nash stares at his son. He opens his mouth like he's going to say something stupid, but then he just nods.

Pilot grabs the back of Nash's jacket and hauls him up. Then he looks at Elton. "Can we make torches like we did the other night?"

Elton hesitates, surprised. "Uh, yeah. Yeah, I guess so."

"Good. Let's get moving, then. I'm tired of these woods."

We all pitch in, adrenaline thumping through our veins.

Soon, we have two torches ready to brave the night. As we duck our heads and crunch into the snow, sidestepping the safety of Elton's fire, I'm feeling torn. On one hand, my body screams for rest. On the other, my heart leaps at the thought that we'll make it to the river tomorrow. Tomorrow! Will I feel my mother's presence there? And is it true that I've had the two things I needed to be an artist all along? How is it that Daddy was so wrong about those words?

Pilot puts a hand on his father's back and gives him something between a pat and a shove. I eyeball Pilot's hands. Wonder what they look like under those gloves. Wonder what Mr. Foster's arm looks like too, and whether his wound will go bad the way Ms. Wade's did.

Another icicle on my heart melts, and a shard of sorrow slams into its place, chewing at my insides. Sucking air between my teeth, I march toward the front and say, "The faster we get there, the faster we'll be warm and fed."

But what I mean is: *The faster we get there, the less likely another of us will lie down in these woods to feed the wolves.*

We walk for a good half hour, every small sound causing us to crane our necks. The smell of smoke tickles my nostrils, and the torches cast a small, safe bubble of light around us.

"We should have done this all along," Elton says. "It's so much colder at night, and it's easier to stay warm this way."

I open my mouth to agree, to make conversation, when I notice Pilot snapping his head to the left and the right. Soon, Mr. Foster is making the same odd, jerking movement, and that basset hound is whining something fierce. They hear something. I cock my own head, raising my good ear and listening and listening and praying I don't hear the thing they do.

But I do.

I hear it, and I know it's coming closer.

CHAPTER
TWENTY-SIX

Pilot and Mr. Foster swing their flickering torches like knights with swords, awaiting a dragon in the darkness. The sound comes from the right, and I twirl in that direction, my gun at the ready.

"Move together," I tell our group. "Shoulder to shoulder."

Nash and Elton close in tight, listening for the breathing, shuffling thing. Or *things*.

My legs grow restless as we wait, the corners of my vision blurring with panic. I place myself in the hunter's position. Decide what it is I'd want most from my prey. Then I say, "Let's keep going. Stay together, but Nash, keep guiding us."

Nash starts forward again. We move slower this time. Take three steps and then listen. Take three more and do it again. After a while, we stop hearing the shuffling and march without pausing. What do we have to fear? We have fire!

We make it another half mile or so before my eyes spot movement. I spin toward the figure I saw, and my heart pounds. I take one tiny step toward the concealed shape. A couple more because Pilot and Mr. Foster may have battle swords, but I have a shiny shield in the form of a thirty-caliber bullet.

"Sloan?" Pilot says, his feet silent against the snow.

I breathe slow and steady, keep my finger on that trigger, and look deep into the woods. I've almost decided I don't see anything other than the trees, when out steps a wolf.

She walks slowly, one foot after another, nose lowered to the ground. Her tail is straight out from her body, the ruff on her neck rigid. Still, I don't miss the fear in her yellow eyes. It's me who's startled her, but that doesn't mean she'll back down. Not with a hungry belly to feed. Not when she doesn't have any other choice.

My body goes numb, and my own eyes widen in awe of this lean, lethal animal. Just a day ago I saw this young gray wolf fight for respect among her pack, and now look at her, facing down a human with new confidence.

The gray wolf growls deep in her throat. A warning. Then she backs up a few steps. Taking her cue, I retreat into Pilot's waiting hands.

He grabs me and yanks me beside him, and I'm so thankful for those hands I could weep.

"Let's go," I whisper. "We have to get out of here."

But before we can take a single step, a different wolf steps into view—the alpha male. He leaps off the ground, excitedly. Nervously. I spot a third wolf, performing the same gesture a few feet away. They seem to be getting each other worked up. Chops are licked and ears are erect and noses are raised.

"Move," I say, not knowing whether that's right and hardly caring. "Go, go!"

Nash takes the first step and we follow, arm against arm, hip against hip. The basset hound scratches at Pilot's leg, and Mr. Foster looks at the dog hard, and somehow—because I am so panic-stricken I'm afraid I may run just to get on with the killing—I know what the man is thinking.

Give them the dog.

I shake the thought from my mind and follow behind Nash, step for step. The wolves follow every movement, whining, growling, yipping. They hate that we're going slow. They want us to run. But I know what will happen if we do. And even though I understand this, I can't stop the twitching in my legs. The bursts of energy in my arms and chest and head that say, *Run, run, run!*

It's something in the way they track us at the edges, trotting and leaping.

Is this the way the rabbits felt?

I moan with fear and follow the group. Elton holds tight to Mr. Foster and Mr. Foster holds tight to him, and Nash moves as fast as he can without breaking into a sprint.

"Get away!" Nash roars.

"Why are they acting that way?" Elton asks, his voice wobbly.

A wolf dashes toward our group, but Pilot is there to greet him. He swings his torch in a great burning arc, and the animal leaps back. A second wolf lunges forward, snapping at Elton's leg, and Mr. Foster charges toward the wolf, his torch granting him courage. The flames touch the wolf on the back, and it yelps. I half expect the wolf to catch fire, but the snow on its back works as armor against the heat.

"We need to run," Nash yells.

"No," I scream. "Stay together! Do *not* run."

My instincts tell me if even one of us flees, then it's over. The wolves will charge, and we'll be divided. Our best bet is to keep their sense of fear stronger than their sense of hunger.

"Keep going," I tell Nash again. "Slow. They'll leave when they see we won't run."

I don't know if I'm right, but it sounds good. When Nash takes another careful step, our group takes it with him. He takes another, and we match it. We're doing well, moving through the snow like a great, slithering monster, our torches two glowing eyes.

Finally, finally, the wolves lose interest. As their excitement wanes, my muscles begin to relax.

"They're going away," Elton says.

Mr. Foster waves his torch back and forth, and though we still see the wolves, they are farther back. Less wild, more watchful. "I believe you're right," he says. "If we just keep going along this way, we'll be okay."

The fire is our protection. A place inside my chest swells remembering that we are man, and they are animal. We create things like fire and torches, and so we win. There is a food chain, even in the heart of these woods.

I think all this with a sense of pride, and relief.

I think all this as I feel the first droplets of rain.

CHAPTER

TWENTY-SEVEN

The sizzle of rain hitting the torches fills me with terror. My lungs tighten around my breath. Pilot glances in my direction, his face a mirror of my own.

It's raining harder.

Water hits the tip of my nose, slides down my jacket, and splatters against my boots.

Elton casts his eyes to the torches. Notes how they dim in the rain.

"What do we do?" the boy yells.

The wolves creep closer, noses to the ground, eyes locked on our twitchy movements. Goose bumps race down every inch of my skin.

"How far until the next shelter?" I ask Nash.

"Too far," he says.

"How far to get back—?"

"Too far!" he roars.

"Should we run?" Elton asks.

"No!" Pilot and I bark at once.

No one says anything. No one moves. I can practically hear our pulses throbbing. We push toward one another, each of us trying to shoulder our way into the center of the group. Into a spot of safety.

But there's no such thing in the woods.

In the rain.

Quietly—so softly I almost don't hear him—Mr. Foster says, "I thought it'd be the cold that killed us."

And then the flames lick out.

Panic buzzes over my entire body. My skin stings, my hands shake so that I can hardly keep ahold of my rifle. I swing it chaotically, forgetting every lesson I've ever learned. Elton screams, but I can't see him. Can't see anything.

As my eyes adjust to the sudden darkness, Pilot grabs my arm. Fumbling, I swivel in the opposite direction and accidently hit Elton with the butt of my rifle. He releases a startled sound as I loop my leg around his.

He understands what I'm doing and grabs on to me with both hands.

"Where are they?" Mr. Foster yells. "Can you see them?"

One second I'm on my feet, the next I'm on the ground.

"It's got my foot!" I scream. The wolf thrashes its head back and forth, my entire body jolting from the movement. Pilot rears back and lands a solid blow into the wolf's side as I slam my rifle into the animal's jawbone.

The wolf releases me with a yelp, but now Elton is screaming.

"I can't find him," Mr. Foster yells. "He's not here!"

I scramble across the snow, feeling the ground, seeing only yellow eyes in the night. Behind me, Pilot makes a strangled noise, and Mr. Foster yells again, only this time it sounds like he's far away.

I hear the snapping of teeth, the urgent rush of paws. And something else. The noise of someone taking flight.

"No!" I yell. "Don't run!"

It feels like kicking a door shut. Like wind rushing across my skin. They've left. The wolves are chasing someone.

Feet scurry across the ground. Paws and boots in one great, chilling flutter of sound. In its place is an emptiness I've known before. My stomach rolls.

"Pilot!" I scream, the sound of my voice jolting me more than wolf teeth on my boot.

When he doesn't respond a million thoughts rush into my mind—

He found me in the woods when I'd given up.

He stayed behind after my father and sister left me.

He reminded me of Sloan the Brave, and I kissed him back.

I scramble to my feet, swinging my gun, horrified that I might be wrong. That the wolves are still here. That I'm the only one left alive and they're saving me for last. I'll never again feel the sunlight on my back as I pull water from our well. I'll never work the summer soil into a harvest, or peel the husk off ripened sweet corn.

And I'll die with this stupid invitation in my pocket!

I hear the sound of Elton some distance away. I scramble over the snow until I find his arms. Yank them up until he's on his feet. His entire body trembles, but he's okay.

"Where's everyone else?" I demand, shaking him by the shoulders. But he doesn't speak. I don't blame him. My voice sounds like it's coming through a microphone, even to my one good ear. If the wolves are still nearby, will making noise call them back?

I drag Elton after me through the pelting rain, my gun balanced in one hand. We walk slowly, afraid to call out anyone's name, afraid not to. Elton clings to me and I cling to him and I've never been so scared in my entire life. Vomit threatens to rise from my throat as my limited vision blurs.

I've decided I can't take another step—not one single step—when I hear Mr. Foster.

"Anyone there?" he whispers.

"We're here," I respond, as loud as I dare. Mr. Foster makes his way over, and we grab arms, thankful we're alive.

"Pilot?" I ask Mr. Foster.

I just barely make out my teacher shaking his head. What does that mean?

What does that mean?!

The wolves howl.

The sound rushes up my ankles, my legs, rises to my neck so that I'm drowning under waves of fear.

"Pilot!" I scream, no longer caring. I have a gun. I have a bullet. I have an aim that's true. "Pilot!"

The wolves howl. They sound close. So close my bottom lip quivers and my ears burn and tears slip down my cheeks because I want my dad and my sister, even if I've disappointed them and they've done the same to me.

And I want my mom. Oh, God. I want my mom!

The pack growls. They're moving closer. Elton's and Mr. Foster's fingers dig farther into my arm, and I wonder if they'll steal my rifle if it comes down to it.

"Sloan?"

A voice in the darkness.

Pilot's voice.

I don't hesitate. I break away from the two at my side and run.

He's squatting beneath a bush when I find him. As if the wolves couldn't smell him out, drag him out. I pull on his leg, but he won't come. I grab his hand and pull, but he doesn't budge.

Panic splits through me as I yank and yank and Pilot doesn't move.

No, my brain fires. *No, no, no!*

I search the snow beneath him, feeling for—what?— blood? Finally, I take his face in my hands and say, "Pilot, say something. Please, please, say something."

His head lolls downward. I open my mouth to scream, but then Pilot Blake opens his and says, "Here."

That's all he gets out, and I don't care. That word is the sun and the moon and the stars. I grab him and haul him to his feet, or as much as I can when he outweighs me by thirty pounds. As soon as he's up, his puppy scampers out from under the bush too. The wolves howl again, and again. Pilot snaps to attention, remembers what's happening.

"Where is everyone else?" he asks.

I shake my head, dread crashing over me because I left Elton and Mr. Foster to find Pilot. Stupid, stupid! Pilot grabs my hand and leaves behind the version of himself that cowered beneath that bush. We race through the woods, through the rain, alarm bells ringing as snow crunches under wolf paws. We need to get back to Elton and Mr. Foster and Nash too, but even more important is learning where exactly those wolves hide. I scan the forest, but I can't see them. I can't see anything!

A human scream rips through the night.

CHAPTER
TWENTY-EIGHT

The scream is loud enough to split the ground wide open. The noise races up my backbone and stops my heart. The wolves answer the cry, but theirs is one of triumph.

They've taken one of us.

The scream comes again and again. It's Elton! No, it's Nash! It's Mr. Foster for sure!

I see two silhouettes. My hand is empty. Where did Pilot go? There! Pilot is safe. Who is he hugging? Elton! I twirl around, searching, searching. And then I see him.

Mr. Foster marches toward us, face twisted in panic, hands over his ears.

Pilot's dog howls in alarm, but it does nothing to mask the sound of those screams. I see it the moment Pilot spots Mr. Foster and realizes—

His father is being attacked by the wolves.

His eyes go big, his hands stretch wide, and his entire body shakes. "Dad!" he screams. "Dad!"

He tries to run, but Mr. Foster is on him in an instant. "No!" his teacher roars. "You stay here."

Pilot tries to break free, but Mr. Foster grabs his face and jerks it close to his own. "You listen to me. Stay put! Do *not* move."

Mr. Foster rushes toward me, and for a moment I'm afraid of this man with his skinny legs and muddy hair. He looks like someone else entirely.

He jerks the rifle from my hands and runs, *runs*, toward the sound of Nash Blake screaming. As he flees into the rain, surrounded by terrible shadows, his color changes from safe, knowledgeable white to brave orange. So orange it burns a hole through the earth, though that can't be right.

Mr. Foster vanishes, and Nash's screams change into something different. As the man moans, Pilot goes from looking like he couldn't move if he wanted to, to racing after Mr. Foster. I'm there to grab him, though it does little to slow him down.

"I have to get to him," he yells, no longer caring about the wolves. "He's my father!"

As I fight against Pilot—knowing no matter what's happened to Nash it's something his son shouldn't see—I realize his dad has stopped making any sounds at all.

A shot rings out.

It's a hundred times louder than any shot I've ever fired. Like the first sound I've heard with both ears in ages.

Pilot drops to his knees, and his dog leaps up to lick his face. He shoves the animal away, and the dog yelps. Sympathy washes over me for the puppy, so I pat him, quick, on the back.

The howling has stopped. The flutter of paws against the snow is gone.

The wolves have fled, but where did that last shot go?

We wait seconds, minutes, days for any noise to reach us.

"Do you hear anything?" I ask Elton, who's come to stand beside Pilot and me.

He shakes his head.

I glance at Pilot, but he's shaking in a different sort of way. Like he knows something bad happened with that shot and it'll change him forever.

When I hear the soft crunch of boots, I'm not sure if it's real, or just hope. But it sounds again, closer, and I know someone's coming.

We wait, the three of us, Elton with his palm in mine, and my other hand touching the crown of Pilot's head.

My heart slows for the first time since we spotted the wolves, and my breath catches in my throat.

The footsteps grow louder.

And Mr. Foster appears. Alone.

He tosses the rifle into the snow as if it burned his hands. He wipes the rain from his face, and when he drops his arms I notice a splattering of something red on his sweater.

"Where is he?" Pilot asks. His question is a knife through my heart. I clench my eyes shut and hope that when I open them again, Pilot's worthless old man will step out from behind Mr. Foster. But I know it isn't happening, so I open my eyes and help Pilot to his feet and nudge his dog toward Elton.

"Mr. Foster?" Pilot says.

My teacher shakes his head, and when he steps closer, I notice he's crying.

Pilot scrunches up his face like he's trying hard not to do the same. His eyes blaze like the torches we lost, and I wonder if he's replacing sadness with anger, just as I replaced my own sadness with numbness.

"Did you shoot one of 'em?" Pilot's voice is so even it scares me more than if he yelled.

Mr. Foster stares at him.

"I asked if you at least got one?" Pilot says.

The man reaches for him. "Pilot—"

Pilot takes a backward step. "Are you sure they got him? It's dark out. He's probably just hurt. Much as I've wished

Nash Blake dead, there isn't a thing in this world that could kill him."

"He's gone," Mr. Foster says without looking up. The words slap me across the face, and even Elton chokes on a sob.

"You don't know what you're talking about." Pilot makes as if he's going to pass by, but the man is there to block his path. As Mr. Foster grabs on to Pilot's arm, the boy explodes like a land mine.

Pilot shoves Mr. Foster and he falls into the snow, rain driving over them both. "Where'd that last bullet *go*? Did you take out the wolf making a meal of my daddy, or did you save it for Nash himself?"

Mr. Foster only crawls to his feet and tries to guide Pilot to him, but Pilot pushes him again. It'd be better if Mr. Foster just said it out loud. That he'd never shoot Nash. Not even if the man was in pain and he thought a bullet was the fastest way to end that pain.

So why doesn't he just say it?

When Pilot goes to shove the man again, or worse, Elton shrieks at him to stop. I grab Pilot by the arms and attempt to drag him back, but it's like wrestling a thunderstorm.

When Pilot pushes me too, I'm so surprised I barely keep myself from falling.

"We've got to get out of here, Pilot," I say, hoping he'll see reason. That he'll remember the wolves are still out there, and that they could return any second. But mostly, I want to stop the look on Pilot's face.

Pilot points at me. "You should have taken that shot. When that wolf got on your boot, you should have shot it. They would have run, and Nash would still be here."

My face burns so hot that my nose, eyes, and ears turn to ash. I open my mouth to reply, to say anything, but I think the heat got my tongue too. He's right. I was saving that bullet. Because, wolf teeth on my boot? That was something I could handle. But what if they'd gone after Pilot? If something happened to him I'd lose my friend, and my lasso.

Every other time the wolves appeared, I had two or more bullets. But tonight, there was only one.

"I'm sorry," I whisper.

"You're sorry?" Pilot says. "My dad is . . . he's . . . You know, if I'd gone ahead to Vernon, my dad wouldn't be out here. I stayed for *you*. I stayed because ever since I brought you out of those woods you've been too scared to do a thing on your own."

Mr. Foster throws his arms around Pilot. To comfort him. To stop the angry words. Pilot struggles against him, and then finally, finally, he allows himself to be embraced. But when the basset hound wiggles out from Elton's hold and runs to Pilot, sensing his owner's distress, Pilot breaks away and stoops to his dog.

He rubs his face with his free hand and glances around, realizing for the first time that we're all still exposed. I can see the fear rushing in to replace the anger.

"Come on," he says, standing up. "You know what my daddy would say if one of you was taken? He'd say we gotta think about ourselves now."

Pilot looks in the direction of where his father must lie, then his eyes fall to the snow and he mutters, "We'll come back for him."

"For both of them," Mr. Foster says quickly.

Pilot winces, and then starts walking. "Let's go."

I glance at my gun. My father's gun. My grandfather's gun. It looks different lying there in the snow, emptied. For all the meals it's brought us, I'm not sure I want it anymore. But it feels odd leaving it behind. That rifle, and my .22, they're a connection to a life my father built. What will I do without a gun in my hands? I give it one last look—recalling the lives that depended on it, and the blood that spilled from its chamber—and I turn toward Pilot.

We follow after him without a word. What else can we do? As we walk through the darkness, not able to see more than five feet ahead, the rain drenching us, I think about Nash Blake and the father he was to Pilot. And I decide, no matter how people live their lives, they leave holes. Because once a person is gone, all that's left is the wondering. Wondering what might have happened if they'd stayed. If things were good, how much more good could there have been? And if things were bad, could they have gotten better?

Now Pilot will never know the answer to that. And neither will I.

We walk another ten minutes before a wolf releases a great and mighty howl in the distance. They've returned to Nash, and we all know it. Pilot stumbles once, and his head drops. Then his back swells as he takes a mighty breath, and he keeps walking.

As I march, I think about all the ice that's gathered on our hearts, and how we'll ever chip it off. And I think about those wolves too. About whether now that they've made a meal of Ms. Wade and Nash too, there's a chance they'll stop there. Because the only thing worse than knowing I've lost another of our group to the woods and the wolves is that those wolves might not be satisfied for long.

But the very worst thought?

The overwhelming, shameful, stomach-turning feeling of thankfulness that the person the wolves are maybe feeding on right this very moment . . . isn't me.

CHAPTER

TWENTY-NINE

We find the final shelter as the sun rises. We just followed the direction Nash had been walking, and kept our eyes peeled for the gashes in tree trunks. Twice, we followed what were probably bear marks. But at last, we stand staring at that tin roof and wood walls and dingy door. After the night we've had, the shelter looks like a mansion.

Elton uses what little strength he has to run ahead. Farts jogs after him, barking at his heels, because apparently there's nothing worse to a dog than a ten-year-old running faster than he is.

Elton disappears inside, and as we close the distance to the shelter, he reappears in the doorway. "Holy moly."

"What is it?" Mr. Foster asks blankly. He's hardly said a word since he vanished between those trees with my rifle, as if the memory of what he did, or didn't do, is too much to bear.

Elton holds his hand above his head. In his grasp is a silver can.

It's food, I realize. *There's food inside the shelter.*

I'm running before I even think to ask how it got there. My body doesn't care about questions. It needs to eat. It needs to sleep. And it needs to shut itself off from my brain, because the memories it holds are too awful to think about.

I rush inside the shelter, Mr. Foster and Pilot directly behind me. Elton is already pushing past us, searching the ground.

"What?" I say, my mouth watering. "What do you need?"

"Rocks," he answers. "Always, rocks."

"What kind?" I ask. "What color?!"

Elton stops his search and looks me straight in the eyes. "A sharp one, Sloan."

I almost smile. Almost.

It takes the four of us under two minutes to find what Elton needs. We practically throw a pile of rocks at his feet.

"This isn't a Boy Scout kind of thing," Elton says, choosing the sharpest rock. "Any of you could do this."

But for some reason, we don't. We stare at Elton as he expertly taps the edge of a can against a larger flat rock as if to loosen the seal. Then he raises the sharp rock and brings it down on the tin top. When it doesn't budge, Elton tries it again. And again. He's grunting from effort when Pilot rips the can and rock from his hand.

Pilot hits it the same way Elton did, but with much more strength. Finally, with a snarl, Pilot hurls it at a nearby tree.

The can bursts open.

Peaches fly through the air and plop into the snow, dripping sticky-sweet down the tree trunk. Farts is the first there, licking the juices with his long, pink dog tongue.

"Oh, gross," Elton says.

But we scramble over anyway, scooping handfuls of half-frozen peaches and snow into our mouths. When there's one questionable-looking slice of peach lying on the ground, no one stops Pilot from taking the honors.

Elton points to the shelter. "There's more."

We don't need encouragement. We're on our feet, racing, stumbling through the snow. Once we get inside, we find he's right. We were too busy worrying over peaches to see that we've been blessed with French green beans, and artichoke hearts swollen with olive oil, and salted potato wedges with skin, and mangoes packed in their own juices, and black-eyed peas and sliced carrots and pickled okra and barbeque baked beans.

And, holy mother of food, there are five cans of potted meat.

We go for the meat first. Grip those pull-tabs, rip off the tops, and dig our fingers inside. The meat is awful. The meat is amazing. The meat is like sunshine on my tongue.

I lick the inside clean after I'm done eating, and open the fifth can for Farts. Pilot sees me doing this, and nods. The weight of his words last night slams into me, but I shove it down because now I've got a can of potatoes and my body is saying *shut up, shut up, shut up* to my brain.

After the potatoes, I reach for the mangoes, breaking the can open and letting the juice run down my throat. We forget the river, we forget the wolves, and we eat until all we can do is lie back, unable to speak, hardly able to draw a breath, as our stomachs stretch toward the sky. Pilot looks over at me, and he takes my hand. His eyes say he's sorry for what he said. Mine say I wish I knew how to ease his pain.

When my mouth grows dry, I stand and whisper to Pilot, "I'm gonna get kindling for a fire so we can melt snow to drink."

He makes as if he'll come with me, but his body moves slowly. I put a hand on his shoulder and add, "I'll be fine."

He nods, and collapses against Elton, who is snoozing alongside Mr. Foster.

Pilot's dog follows me as I walk, making me feel less

alone in my search. I don't find any dry bark, but I do chance upon a rock I think Elton can use. I'm clawing at a rotted tree when the basset hound suddenly races ahead, cutting a quick path in the snow. Everything in my body wants me to return to Mr. Foster and Elton and Pilot. But I can't go back without the dog. So I shove the rock in my pocket, and I sprint after him.

Farts runs faster, and I realize he's chasing a squirrel. Idiot.

"Farts, get over here."

The squirrel dashes into a hole in the ground, and the basset hound goes nuts, howling as if someone cut off those long, goofy ears. He races to the hole and scratches at the entrance, trying to get inside.

"I see you're brave when it comes to squirrels," I say, bending to corral him. I stop when my fingers brush barbed wire. I follow the wire to a wooden stake and realize what it is I'm touching.

My father's fence. The one he and his men built. I wrap my hands around the wire, careful to mind the barbs, and move it back and forth. Slowly. And then faster. Frustration simmers inside me as I yank harder and harder, trying to— what?—to take down at least a small piece of this ridiculous fence? This fence that helped put us in harm's way. And why? Because my father said it would help?

I believed him. I thought he knew all about hunting. But he doesn't know everything. Neither did my mom.

I dig my heels into the snow and lean back, shake even harder.

I love my parents. But they don't always know what's best, which means someday I'm going to have to learn to trust myself.

"Argh!" I yell, releasing the fence.

Farts dashes away from me and into a thicket, deciding with his large dog brain that the squirrel didn't go in the hole after all. Or maybe he's running from my meltdown. Who knows?

"No, get back here. Come on, we gotta go."

The puppy backs up. Slowly. Too slowly. He whines and tucks his tail and shoots a nervous look in my direction.

Every muscle in my body grows stiff. The dog lowers his head and hesitates for one long moment.

Then he bolts.

A wolf, the alpha male, springs from the thicket and chases Pilot's dog.

I don't know what makes me do it—the thought of watching the dog die or imagining Pilot's face or because my parents aren't always right or because I don't know, I don't know—but I lunge in front of the wolf and scream, "No!"

Farts disappears into the distance, and the wolf halts

because he hadn't seen me, but now here I am. Without a rifle. Without anything but my own racing heart and enough meat on my bones to feed this animal.

The wolf charges, bloodlust in his yellow eyes, and I run.

I don't make it two feet before there's a flutter of movement.

A snowshoe hare rushes from the hole in the ground, startled by the squirrel and driven mad by the scent of wolf. The rabbit thinks it can make it too.

The rabbit is wrong.

The wolf dashes toward it, a snarling hunter. His jaws close down over the hare and he lifts his wriggling, screaming prize.

As the animal lopes into the woods, I run back toward the shelter. I only make it a short distance when I hear Elton calling my name. The relief at hearing him brings a smile to my face.

"I'm here," I yell, still running. "There was a wolf!"

I'm almost laughing with joy at being alive—the sun on my head and the snow underfoot and the pleasure of food in my belly—when I hear Mr. Foster holler.

"Look out!" he screams.

I hear a snarling that I know comes from more than one wolf. The rest of the pack is here.

I make it through the brush in time to see Mr. Foster

running toward Elton. He screams, and the sound breaks my skull into a billion jagged pieces.

Mr. Foster doesn't make it to him in time.

But he does run fast enough to draw the wolves' attention away from Elton.

The first wolf lunges at Mr. Foster.

But it's the second one that kills him.

CHAPTER THIRTY

This time, no one tells us not to run. We'd do it anyway. Our boots dash through the snow as Pilot ensures his dog stays close and my left eye twitches and Elton cries, panicked after Mr. Foster fell. We dive over bushes and rush around trees and haul each other off the ground when one of us trips.

We do not speak.

We just run.

A wolf howls in the distance, and we zip forward. As we race onward, in shock, in fear, a memory seizes my mind. My mother bartering for fertilized eggs. Those eggs becoming chicks. And finally, one winter day, those chickens lying slaughtered in the snow.

A fox, my father said. *When they get desperate, they kill more than they need.*

Are wolves the same? I wonder now, my brain buzzing with hysteria. *They've taken Ms. Wade. And Nash Blake. And Mr. Foster. Will they stop?*

They'll never stop!

I run faster. Can barely catch my breath. Can hear them coming. No, it's my imagination.

Or is it?

Up ahead there's a fallen tree. It's enormous. Too large to crawl over quickly. The perfect size for a wolf to leap over with ease. They're going to get us. We don't stand a chance.

"Go around," Elton yells.

"No, go under. Look, there's a hole!" Pilot replies.

We run, and then I know without a shadow of a doubt that I *do* hear the wolves.

When Pilot speaks again, his voice is pure panic. "Go under, Elton. Go, go, go!"

Elton doesn't need to be told again. He flies toward the tree, eyeing both ends, still wondering if it'd be faster to run around instead. No. Pilot's right. He has to do as he's told.

Elton slides onto his belly like a batter going for home. He gets stuck halfway, but wriggles frantically until he's on the other side.

I wait for Pilot to go ahead, but he shoves me toward the fallen tree. "Go under! Hurry, Sloan!"

The wolves howl. They're so close. They're right behind us.

"No, Pilot!" I scream, tears in my voice. "You first. You go first!"

But Elton grabs my ankles and pulls and Pilot shoves

my shoulders and screams something, I don't know what, and then I'm halfway beneath the tree and now I can barely see him.

I can't see my person my lasso my Pilot!

I'm half-deaf but I hear it when the wolves catch up. When they find Pilot all alone. I see it when Pilot falls on his stomach and crawls toward us. And I feel it when I grab his hands and yank hard, hard, hard but not hard enough.

The wolves pull him backward.

He disappears from sight.

A wolf growls and makes a sound like it's launching itself forward. But then there's a new sound. A snarl so unlike those wolves. It takes me a moment. Then I know. It's Pilot's dog.

Elton tugs on my arm, saying we have to go. We have to. But I'm frozen. If I go back under that tree, I'm dead. If I stay here, I'm dead.

The dog's snarls grow brave and bold, like he's been afraid every day of his short dog life but those wolves are *not* taking his person. Pilot yells and I know that the dog is fighting a wolf.

Pilot's dog yelps.

Pilot screams.

I throw myself beneath the tree, desperate to help, and my heart explodes from my chest.

A wolf stares at me. Mere inches away.

I scream and wiggle backward. The wolf tries to crawl after me, but decides halfway to return to Pilot and the basset hound. Once I'm on my feet, I glance at where I last saw Elton. But he's gone.

CHAPTER

THiRTY—ONE

I fly through the snow, following Elton's footprints, knowing I must get to him before the wolves do. Knowing the two of us have to stay together to stand a chance. I follow his footsteps, but somehow, someway, his tracks vanish. The snow has returned, quietly, sneakily. Maybe his tracks were covered. But no, that's not possible. Not that fast.

Crazy with fear, I stop searching for Elton and simply *run*. Because I heard the way Pilot screamed. It was the same sound his daddy made. The sound Mr. Foster would have if given the chance.

Pilot is . . . he's . . .

No.

No, no, no!

I have to go back.

I have to find the river.

I have to die out here as I was always meant to.

I stumble to a stop and crouch down. Press my hands to

the snow. If only I had my gun. If only I had my father, sister, mother, lasso. I need something to help me survive. But I have nothing. I am only me—

Sloan Reilly.

And that is not enough. I can't fight a single wolf, much less a pack. These animals will hunt me, chase me, crunch on my bones. Will they leave anything at all?

Tears flow, and I breathe so fast I can't fill my lungs. I may suffocate before they find me.

Where is Elton? I think suddenly. *Do they have him already?*

No, he's a smart kid. He'll find the river.

He has to.

I have to.

I take a few tentative steps, and I listen. Try to hear Elton or the dog or a wolf. There's nothing. But I *can* hear the subtle rush of . . . something.

The river?

THE RIVER!

I grab my knees, hunch over, suck in oxygen. Can't get enough. Have to stop. Can't stop. I've got to run, but my body won't cooperate. The echo of Pilot's scream rings through my head, and I stand upright. I have to get to my father, who can keep me safe. Who will never force me to be alone again.

Alone.

I'm alone.

Except for the woods and the snow . . . and the wolves. They are here to keep me company, just as they were two years ago.

A snapping sound reaches my ear.

Just the good one. Just the right one.

It's that same young gray female. The one who's been hunting us, keeping her pack on our trail, all this time.

She strides closer, teeth bared, two good ears to track every move I make. She looks at me with gold eyes that seem to say—

Blood. Blood, blood, blood, blood, blood.

CHAPTER
THIRTY-TWO

As the wolf stalks toward me, I notice there's red smeared on her muzzle. She's already made a kill, but it wasn't enough.

She stops at the perimeter of where I stand—a small clearing surrounded by soaring red alders.

I suppose that's it then. A chill rushes over my skin as I watch the wolf watching me. The memory of those two wolves tracking that rabbit invades my mind once again, and I'm filled with that same dread.

My legs itch to run, but instead I take one small step back and nearly trip over something in the snow.

The wolf growls.

It's easier to give up than I imagined it'd be. I have no hope of fighting this animal. If she wants me, I am hers. A strange calmness settles over my shoulders.

I'm crippled with sadness from the loss of people I love, and the thought of going on without Ms. Wade's no-nonsense loving care, or Mr. Foster's passion for knowledge, or my mother's soft hands in my hair and her lips on my forehead and her arms around me saying, *You can go and be anything, anything.*

And I am crippled by the thought of going forward without Pilot. Who made it seem as though I could survive it all as long as he was nearby.

But those people are gone. And as for me—

Well, I guess I was always meant to die in these woods.

As the gray wolf takes a step in my direction, I close my eyes. I will not give her the satisfaction of running me down. I will stand here, my feet firm in the snow, and I will find a good place in my mind to go.

I hear the soft crunching as she comes closer.

How quiet she is.

I breathe in, I breathe out, and though my body shakes so hard I'm afraid I may collapse, I keep my eyes cinched shut and I block out the world. Use that same ice that once covered my heart to cover my entire self. And there, behind my eyes, I allow my entire life to blaze forth.

I recall my father teaching me how to hold a rifle, the butt firm against my shoulder. His callused hands are strong around mine, and I imagine that with him here, and this heavy gun in my control, nothing bad could ever happen.

I remember one afternoon when Maren dressed me in my mother's nightgown and painted our faces with mud.

We danced in the rain and stole carrots from our neighbor's garden and used them as swords against invisible enemies.

I remember the first time I realized Pilot had grown big. The way he smiled at me—old friends who hadn't spoken in years—and how everything my mother told me about crushes became interesting.

I remember when my mother recognized the art in me, and so she made me stand before her painting and I saw blue and blue and blue. And then she made me stand real close, and suddenly—a rainbow of colors hidden within all that blue, like magic! And now, for whatever reason, I wonder about that painting and those secret colors.

I wonder too if I could capture more dark and light in the world using nature, and do something well other than shooting.

I wonder what I'd see if I went to Anchorage and entered that competition.

I wonder if I could leave Rusic and live a big, loud, unafraid life and make new memories.

Something snaps in my brain. And I remember that I was once brave. That I am *still* brave. I demanded we get help for Ms. Wade and I punched Nash Blake in the nose and I shot the wolf that almost killed Elton. I kissed Pilot and I walked across the frozen river first.

I made my way to the river. I made it! The old Sloan is

here, right where I left her. And I am here too—a yellow girl who isn't as yellow as I thought.

And Elton, he wasn't yellow when he admitted he was lonely, was he? And Pilot, he wasn't orange after he lost his daddy. And my own daddy wasn't green when he hugged me so hard after Mama left—just the once—that I felt the bones in his rib cage.

Mr. Foster and Nash and Ms. Wade, they're like Mama's painting. All those secret colors beneath one big, bold hue.

I figured I was yellow.

I figured wrong.

I am a rainbow of courage and fear, of sadness and hope, of vulnerability and intuition.

I am a painter's palette of colors. And now I'm standing here, waiting for death and refusing to run because I am brave and just because you're scared for a little while doesn't mean you have to be scared forever.

My eyes flick open, and I see that lethal animal standing a mere three feet away. I look into the face of the wolf and I think—

I want to live!

I want to live and see and do and be anything, anything!

The exact moment I decide this, is the exact moment the wolf attacks.

But she doesn't know Sloan the Brave.

Sloan the Brave was born to fight.

CHAPTER

THiRTY-THREE

I take a defiant step toward the wolf, and she halts, confused. "Come and get me!" I scream, taking a second step. My boot hits the thing it did earlier, and I glance down to find a branch lying in the snow. Perfect for one of Elton's torches.

Or for a weapon.

I grab it and swing hard. Blood pumps through my veins and my heart rages and though my arms shake from adrenaline and—yes, okay—fear, I'm able to hold that branch steady.

I don't wait for the wolf to launch another attack. Releasing a wild cry, I sprint toward her.

"I don't run from you," I roar. "You run from *me*!"

The wolf darts out of the way, and I swing again, swirling in great circles, my mouth open to the falling snow. I howl, savage, like the wolves until my voice grows hoarse.

The animal seems uncertain of how to react. She's threatened, and hungry, so the hair rises on her neck and her lips pull back from her teeth in vicious growls. But she also seems tensed to flee.

I allow this sliver of optimism to slip inside right as the gray wolf latches on to my branch. She takes the thing between those powerful jaws and snaps her head back and forth. She growls, digs her back legs into the ground, pulls backward.

My fingers lose their grip and the branch soars from my hand. I fall onto my rear, which I know is bad. She springs forward, snarling.

I leap to my feet and kick, but the gray wolf keeps coming. For one horrible second, I believe I'll die moments after I realized I wanted to live. She dashes ahead, growling murderously, tired of playing games. Her teeth sink into my leg as my world blazes with heat and pain and terror and color. *Red.*

"No!" I yell, because I don't want this. I don't want to be eaten. "No, no!"

I lean back, and with my free leg, I smash the animal in the face. It takes four strong kicks before the wolf releases her hold.

I struggle to my feet, but the wolf is there in an instant. She bites down on my forearm and pulls with those lean legs. The animal wants me on the ground. I can see her eyes on my face, driven by primal urges to open my throat. I know this because I am a hunter too.

I reach into my pocket and grab the stone I found for Elton. Mustering every ounce of strength I have remaining, knowing this is my last stand, I grip that rock and I slam it into the gray wolf's nose. I hit her again and again, screaming in her face, and finally the wolf breaks away with a yelp.

I stumble from the absence of her weight, and something drops from my pocket. It's the art invitation, dislodged when I grabbed the stone. The young wolf takes it into her teeth and I snatch the other side. I pull, leaving the corner in her mouth.

"No, you can't have it!" I roar at her.

Jamming it back into my pocket, I hobble toward the branch and take it into my hands, dripping blood from my calf and arm. This time though, I don't swing. I simply hold it there against me in a show of controlled power. The wolf grows uneasy at the sight of that branch. I stare her in the eyes and gasp to catch my breath, and I tell her with my posture, my human head held high—

I am not easy prey.

I am strong.

I fill my lungs and square my shoulders and make myself appear as large as possible. And then I do the thing that makes my legs shake beneath me—

I turn my eyes away from the wolf.

I am unafraid. I am unbeatable.

You are not a threat.

I take a small step away from the wolf, keeping my body turned to the side so as not to show her my back. When she doesn't immediately attack, I take a second step.

I take a third step. A fourth. And by the time I lose track of how many slow steps it's been, I know that the wolf has given up, and that I have won. I look back only once and see her watching me. We stare into each other's eyes, and something unnamable passes between us. Eventually, the wolf grows bored, and turns to trot away.

And that is how my dance with death ends. Not with wild cries or cutting stones or swinging fists. But with the whisper of wolf feet against the snow.

CHAPTER
THIRTY—FOUR

Once I regain control of my senses, I hear the river. The hum of the water increases as I move closer. I have to grit my teeth against the pain spreading up and down my right side, but I keep going, keep pushing.

Finally, I see the wide-open stretch of sky. It's all here— the rocky bank, the water, the boat. It looks exactly the way it did two years ago, except I'm not the same girl I was then. And I never will be again. But that doesn't have to be a bad thing.

I stumble twice as I run toward the water. My head throbs, and my vision is blurry, but as I get closer I know I'm not imagining things.

There in the boat is Elton Dean Von Anders. He's already working his Boy Scout hands over the engine, pulling that cord over and over. He wipes his brow and tries again.

"Elton," I say, but he doesn't hear me. I stand upright and try to repeat his name, but sorrow closes my throat.

I thought I'd lost him like I lost Pilot. Like I lost Mr. Foster and Ms. Wade and my mother. I cover the wound on my arm and open my mouth to speak again.

That's when I hear his voice.

"I couldn't find her," he says. "I looked—"

We see each other in the same moment.

He looks at me, those warm brown eyes. That same blond buzz cut and shoulders growing wide. But there's something different about him. The lasso around his waist is gone.

I don't need it anymore.

But I still need him.

My friend.

Pilot drops whatever he's holding and we rush toward each other, the snow falling over our heads. He grabs my shoulders and I wince.

"Are you okay?" he asks, his voice louder than it needs to be. He has a gash on his face, but that's all right. If you live in Rusic, you learn to love scars. I love them already. "Sloan, say something," he commands. "Sloan!"

I swallow, lean against him because I can't believe we made it. Can't believe he's here and one day I can show him how to hold a rifle and maybe one day he'll kiss me again and we can be there for each other to lean on because that's how it's supposed to be.

My heart sings and my mouth turns upward in a tired smile. "Here," I say. "I'm here."

Pilot guides me toward the boat, and I hold on to every question I have for him, like how he got away, and what happened on the other side of that fallen tree. One look in his eyes says he has questions for me too. But we focus on boarding the boat, and on Elton throwing his arms around me, saying he knew I was too stubborn to die, and did I see how brave he was back there?

I almost laugh. But then I notice something, and it breaks a piece of this hopeful ending we're making.

"Pilot, where's your dog?"

Pilot lowers his eyes, and slowly shakes his head. He tries to speak, but in the end, it's Elton who steps forward and pats Pilot on the shoulder, saying, "That dog was brave in the end. That's all that matters. He's a hero, that stinky dog."

Pilot wipes away a tear. "Let me try the motor."

I sit down, sorry all over again at the loss of that basset hound. He wasn't my dog. But he was one of us. And he saved Pilot. I'll never forget him.

My heart twists as the motor on Mr. Clive's boat springs to life. As we move gently away from the bank, I gaze ahead. I decide I will enter that art competition. I will forget about my lasso. I will feel fear again, but when I do, I'll remember that fear can be overcome.

I will live big and loud and brave because I walked through the woods twice, and I was stronger the second time through.

As Pilot steers the boat, I look at the woods once more. To say goodbye. To hold my chin to the sky and be proud.

But instead all I can focus on is the swiftly moving blob racing along the shore.

"Is that what I think it is?" Elton asks.

Pilot turns and sees what Elton and I do.

Farts races through the snow, legs flying, floppy ears swinging. He runs faster than I've ever seen a dog run. When he sees that we see him, he barks once, sharply, and then turns toward the water, and without pause, he dives into the river.

Pilot laughs like I haven't heard him in years, and he pulls Farts from the freezing water and covers him with his jacket. "Dumb dog," he says. "You dumb, dumb dog."

Elton sighs with relief, clearly overjoyed, but says only, "Can we go now?"

I scratch the basset hound behind his ears and smile up at Pilot. I'm glad that we can smile at all after everything we've been through. We will never forget the lives lost in these woods. But if we can smile now, even for a moment, then we can find happiness at the end of this. I just know it.

As the boat moves toward the center of the river, and we

chug through the icy water, I imagine for a second that I see the slim body of a wolf racing through the trees. From my place between Pilot and Elton, the animal looks beautiful, magnificent. A beast of the wild, not so unlike myself.

I imagine the wolf howls.

But if it does, I can no longer hear it.

AUTHOR'S NOTE

The idea for this book was forged from a storm. And a dream. As a brutal wave of snow and freezing temperatures rocked the northeastern coast of the U.S. I sat warm in my bed. New Yorkers dashed to grocery stores, buying out bottled water and canned goods and matches. Living in Texas, I couldn't imagine preparing for a winter storm of this proportion.

I turned off the lamp that night, thinking about the cold. The snow. About what would happen to all those people if it never let up. Then I slept. And I dreamed. And in my dreams, the wolves came. A blizzard raged too long. And those wolves grew hungry. They had nothing to eat because skyscrapers and condo buildings and parking lots had swallowed their land, and their food. So a-hunting they did go.

When I woke, I couldn't stop thinking of those wolves. So I took a drive to my family's cabin in Blanco, Texas, where I spent my youth unearthing Comanche arrowheads and learning how to fire a rifle. The one-room cabin sits on two hundred acres of family-owned land, is heated by a generator on cold winter nights, and has a potbellied stove in the center of the room. There, on a porch built by my grandfather, the Moleskine notebook in my lap lit by a kerosene lamp, I fleshed out the first scenes for what would later become *Hear the Wolves*.

As part of my research for this novel, I drove to a wolf sanctuary two hundred miles from my home. Regardless of what previous conceptions I may have held before arriving, I soon learned that wolves are *not* dogs. They cannot be tamed, and will never think of humans as their masters. In other words, mind your fingers.

As I strolled toward the building, I saw the difference for myself. Two wolves watched me from behind a chain-link fence. They'd spotted me long before I'd seen them. Grizzled in color, and lean, they tracked my every movement, quietly. No barking. No running. They simply watched.

I'd be lying if I said it didn't unnerve me.

Soon after, I was kindly shown inside the office and asked to sign paperwork instructing me not to bend down. Or look a wolf in the eye. Or wear sunglasses. Or run.

The list went on.

"This is a lot of stuff to remember," I said to my tour guide, with a nervous laugh.

"We'll make sure you're okay," he replied. "Most of this is just to ensure you don't scare the wolves."

We went through two locked gates to arrive in the first spacious enclosure. And I discovered that while the wolves were affectionate and respectful of the handlers they'd grown to trust, I was an unknown. They kept their distance, always watchful, always quiet. Until of course, I ventured too close on our way out. A large male growled deep in his throat. An unmistakable warning. My guide stepped in, and I swiftly made my exit.

After my first close encounter, the deeply knowledgeable guide walked me past numerous enclosures, talking about the wolves, answering my plethora of questions. Finally, he looked at one of the handlers and asked, "Should she meet Achilles?"

Who is Achilles? I thought. *I don't want to meet Achilles.*

The handler shrugged. "Yeah, I think it'd be fine. We're still working with him, but we'll all go in with her."

"Achilles is new," the guide said, looking at me. "He's . . . large."

I don't wanna meet Achilles, I don't wanna meet Achilles, I don't wanna meet Achilles.

"Cool," I said. "Let's do it."

With a trainer on one side of me, and my guide on the other, I followed a second trainer into Achilles's enclosure.

The wolf trotted toward us quickly. We leaned against the cage, not moving, not speaking. Achilles smelled my hands, my legs, my crotch. My heart beat so hard I thought I might faint. I didn't realize how large wolves could get until this moment. I didn't realize how large their teeth were.

"He'll be even bigger in the winter," one of the handlers told me.

But I could hardly focus on what she was saying, because all I was thinking was, *I forgot to take off my sunglasses. The wolf is going to maul me because I forgot to remove my sunglasses!*

But Achilles was surprisingly generous and playful. So when the female handler suggested I take a photo next to him, I agreed . . . after ensuring the male handler would stay close by. As I posed with the wolf, I made the mistake of placing my hand on top of his head. A big no-no. The handlers had told me as much. A mouthing from Achilles redirected my hand, and I made my exit soon after.

On our way back to the office, I snapped pictures of the encaged wolves. One too many, I suppose. A large female grew visibly agitated before leaping toward the chain-link fence with a growl. The guide drew me back and told me it was the snapping of my camera that had frightened her. I apologized and went to pocket the thing, wondering if I was in over my head. Trying to recall how many hours I was from home.

But then something happened.

A wolf began to howl.

Soon after, another joined in. And then . . . magic. Every last wolf in the sanctuary erupted in howls, noses to the sky, long, mournful wails blending. Each had their own unique sound, but somehow, they still created a harmonic chorus that'll keep me dreaming of wolves long after this book reaches readers.

My visit to the sanctuary taught me many things. First, how blessed the resident animals are to have such respectful, compassionate, committed caretakers. But mostly, what I learned is that humans threaten the lives of wolves much, *much* more than wolves do us. In fact, for the amount of fear we hold toward wolves, there hasn't been a fatal attack on a human in North America since 2010.

That's not to say wolves never pose a danger. They do have quite the history, after all. According to my research, and that of others (especially *The Fear of Wolves: A Review of Wolf Attacks on Humans*, 2002), there were approximately 1,572 wolf attacks on humans in the eighteenth century, 2,509 attacks in the nineteenth century, 703 attacks between 1900 and 1949, and 1,150 attacks between 1950 and 2000. These numbers include incidents recorded by reliable sources only, so it's reasonable to assume the actual number of attacks may be significantly higher.

Wolf attacks are generally clustered in time and location, meaning once a wolf, or wolf pack, has deemed humans a possible food source, they will continue hunting them until the wolves are killed. For example, in 1995, seventy-five children were attacked in a localized area of India over a period of only eight months. Compare that to the one North American death in the past five years.

One of the attacks in India provided the story Nash retells about a child taken before her mother's eyes, leaving only the head for authorities to find. As much as I tried to find proof that the story was fabricated, it appears it actually happened.

As I purchased a wolf plush for my daughter, my guide sheepishly asked me about my book. I explained the story, and his face fell. "Oh, so they *are* bad wolves," he said, visibly disappointed. "Not exactly," I explained. "See, the humans took away their normal food source. And they built a fence that blocked other prey. Also, the wolves live really close to the residents, so they don't fear them." These are all things he'd told me increased the chances of wolf attacks, and I knew from research that wolves living near campsites and national parks have had aggressive run-ins with campers due to proximity and a lack of negative conditioning.

The more comfortable wolves grow with humans, and the

more they associate them with food, the more likely they are to attack, he'd explained earlier.

I finished the premise for the story, and asked, "So, is it totally irrational to think these Alaskan wolves would attack my characters?"

"Well, no," he answered honestly. "Actually, it's that certain situation I was telling you about. It could happen."

On my way out, the female handler waved cheerfully. "You know, I'm a photographer. If you want to come back in winter, I'll get a shot of just you and Achilles in the field. He'll have his winter coat, so he'll be *huge*. Just the two of you this time!"

"Sounds great!" I chirped.

I haven't taken her up on the offer.

Would you?

Photograph by Victoria Scott

ACKNOWLEDGMENTS

I'm thankful to so many people who loved, shaped, and rallied behind *Hear the Wolves*.

To my agent, Sara Crowe, who instantly championed the idea. To the team at Scholastic—Erin Black, the only person who could rival the passion I have for *Hear the Wolves*; Nina Goffi, for a cover that brought me to tears; as well as to Michelle Campbell, Saraciea Fennell, Lauren Festa, Emily Heddleson, Lizette Serrano, Tracy Van Straaten, Elizabeth Tiffany, and the domestic and foreign sales teams. And I couldn't forget Nikki Mutch; thank you for being a fantastic fan.

To my family and friends for continually asking what I'm working on next, especially Mark Stanley, my dad, the ultimate outdoorsman, who read this book before anyone else and provided invaluable feedback on all things hunting, wildlife, and weaponry. And to author pal April Genevieve Tucholke, who was reading an early version of this book at night, while her husband was away, and had to put it down until he returned. Are those coyotes still lurking?

To my daughter, who reminds me there are things worth fighting and growing for, and finally, always, to my husband. You believed in this book. You believed in *me*. By the time you read this we'll be across the country. To our next great adventure!